# Two
# Saints
# City

*Miles Venn*

Get a Grip Publishers

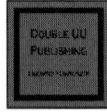

1st published in 2024

# Table of Contents:

¼ WAY THROUGH: PAGE 60

½ WAY THROUGH: PAGE 120

¾ WAY THROUGH: PAGE 154

LAST CHAPTER: PAGE 200

*"Fuck or get fucked."*

— **Razor Lip Henson**

*"Men who kill are unbound by social convention and should therefore forego the societal protection."*

— **The Honorable Judge Thourne**

*"Be the creature that you are or live as a mimic. But don't expect the tiger's due just because you wear stripes."*

— **Sidney Gorealte**

# 1.

I've been hard on life. Yeah, I was born blue-collar poor, but I fell in with the wrong people and kicked around on the wrong side of the tracks by choice. I never made any real effort to cross over, to pull myself up by the steel toe bootstraps. I thought I was better than the ordinary struggle, I thought life owed someone special like me a favor. Life, my friend, it don't give a shit.

The struggle: with an investment of time and effort, life rewards hard work, but hard work mostly pays out small. Hard work is hand to mouth, scrimp and save, unpaid bills and never-never installments: installments of relief, installments of joy, installments of success, and installments of failure.

I never planned to live life in installments. Truth is, I never really planned for any future at all, I just hit life head-on, and life hit back with a left hook counter that stunned my perception. I got up from the canvas angry. It don't matter who's in your corner between rounds, when the fight's on you gotta defend yourself at all times, keep your opponent on the back foot, and pummel the motherfucker when they're on the ropes. Sometimes the opponent is life itself, sometimes it's every fucker else, and sometimes it's your own ego you're fighting against—I fought 'em all, and it don't stop, not really, even after you retire, so keep swinging.

Most egos have a higher opinion of themselves than is justified. Even if an egotist makes it big, the ego thinks it's more important than it is, smarter than it is, a better prospect than it is, maybe more so for those who can justify their actions by the measure of their achievements—even at the expense of lesser egos. The ego's a fat fuck that feeds on success and resentment and narcissism. And when life fails to deliver on the calorific promises the ego stuffs into its face, the conceited fat bastard looks for excuses why it's waddling behind rather than sprinting ahead.

I'm no different, I judge others with a lean attitude that sizes-up the girth of their flaws. And that's what this story's about, trimming the rind and serving up the meat of who I am, what I do, and what I've done.

After flunking outta high school I slip into an 'easy money' way of life. I was big and plenty tough for door security work by night and boxing by day. I take a few pro fights, was invited to the sparring camps of some top-level boxers who use me as a warmup punching bag before their fights. I could've made better use of my pro card. With time and consistency and endurance training, I was good enough to make a living fighting, not mansion house and tigers on the tennis court money, but enough to finance me until I aged outta the fight game. Instead, I took the quick money option, getting paid thug wages for bouncing heads off pavements outside clubs and bars, or bouncing threats off the imprudent skulls of numbskulls who owed other people pain or payment. My skull took a metal bar to the brow, not hard enough to crush bone, but it split my left eyebrow open vertically: that totally avoidable injury nixed my availability for paid sparring for 2 months and, as a result, my career hit the ropes and so did my legit earnings.

2 months is a long time to go hungry, to sleep in your car. I had no savings to fall back on, had no credit for a bank loan, I was on the verge of having to find an honest job—I didn't even look for one. For a while, I still paid taxes on the door security work I did, but the flesh on the bones of my scrawny income came from non-tax-deductible sources.

There are reasons why men like me exist, all of them bad, and all of them down to who we are rather than the system, or our upbringing, or the chip on our shoulders. Men like me are wrong and we make wrong choices every day. I know this. I'll admit responsibility. I'm not capable of character change, my arc has flatlined, so I'll own my flaws like a trademark.

The dark euphemisms we use to describe the things we do in the shady trade of underworld collection and distribution is a sidestep that talks around the fact that we put the hurt on people for money, which I don't got a problem with considering the species of scum I generally distribute hurt to. If you got a problem with that, maybe this ain't a read for you?

Like I say, my current situation is not my choice. Well, that's not strictly true, I did choose not to stack pallets in a warehouse or drive a fucking van for fucking Amazon to earn a living—I'm tough, but I ain't that tough.

My name? Saint Greaves, and, yeah, I hear the irony in that. The reason behind my christened name can be traced back to my mad Irish Catholic mother, who loves the Holy Trinity more than she does her 4 kids.

Me? I got the Holy Spirit beaten outta me at a young age by the biological conduit that is my mother. She'd invoke God's forgiveness as she was pulling my hair or smacking me around—she even made my old man give me the belt when he got home from work as a kinda dessert after she'd served up her starters and main course of abuse. And then I'd be expected to confess the sins I'd taken a beating for in the week at church after mass, so some frock-wearing rosery botherer could dish out Hail Mary's and Our Father's like pious shin kicks that make you kneel. Kneeling: it's just as tough on the ego as it is on the knees, I spent my life avoiding that pain.

I got 2 older brothers—Diligence Greaves and Concord Greaves, and a younger sister—Chastity Greaves. Needless to say, my brothers and sister's names got shortened to Dil, Con, and Chas. Me? I was fucking lumbered until some wiseass started calling me Halo, and that kinda stuck.

So, I got a past I ain't especially proud of, and my future looks like more of the same, but I make the most of it. I got myself a 3-year jolt in Menard Correctional Center and Hill's for assault and battery. I did my time without bitching, grateful that the 2 homicides I was sought in connection with, which were technically self-defense, were dropped by the DA's office through lack of evidence. Admittedly, I did preemptively defend myself in 1 case before my attacker got into offensive position. And the other case was a 50/50 sorta deal, but both happened in the pursuit of criminal enterprise. There are 3 more homicides that the cops never got wind of. I can't claim self-defense for those, they were straight-up murder.

Falling foul of the law and losing a steady income stream was only a short hop over the fence into full-time lawbreaking and leg-breaking to make ends meet. When I should've knuckled down and taken the hit of ordinary life, I shifted into a strange, what would you call it? ... alternative economic existence, where most people I come across know me by my nickname 'Halo' along with some dubious IDs I'd acquired on the street. After a couple of jobs bruising my knuckles reminding a mark of their debt obligation, I start bringing equipment in a leather grip tool bag to speed things along. You'd be surprised, or maybe you wouldn't, how quickly an IOU gets paid when the ballpeen hammer comes out.

I like grip bags: not too bulky, easy to throw shit into and carry around, fits in the trunk of a car without annoying corners making a Tetris puzzle outta packing. Also, every damn thing I own can be packed and shifted from place to place in a fair-sized, durable polyester carryall luggage grip—but '2 Grips' as an AKA don't sound as cool or trip off the tongue as my Saintly handle.

Even before my full-time criminal activities scattered any legit career path with broken glass evidence and push-tack arrest warrants, I kept things simple. After my 1st and last permanent girlfriend cheated on me when I was serving a stretch, I dropped outta the relationship game. I still get horny, but now I scratch that itch with hookups and call girls—escorts, I mean. After I lost my 1st rented apartment, because you can't earn 3 years of rent and buy commissary in the tiers, living arrangements became merely temporary. Losing most of my shit brought me to a pragmatic revelation, I discovered I ain't an emotionally materialistic person when it comes to possessions—but I don't got much to be possessive over, so…?

When you can make do or do without, you don't want for much. But the little I do want I won't compromise on. What do I want? I don't get overly attached to the car I drive: I can walk away and catch a bus if a ride gets too hot. I don't get overly committed to the guns I shoot: I can strip a weapon down, clean off my finger dabs, and throw it in the river if CSI ballistics washes off the blood and brain matter and records on their database the rifling on a bullet I've spent. I got a 1 item, a family heirloom you might call it, that I'd be pissed to lose, but I'd be more pissed at losing my freedom, so I'd let that go if I needed to.

I got a medium-game plan in mind, but there's linebacker obstacles I need to clear before I can get outta the pain business and into the pleasure business of retirement. Sports metaphors, though, have a price if you wanna drive the ball over the touchline: what that price is depends on what you want and how you plan to get it...and whether you're willing to pay.

Cash is an iron that can smooth out all wrinkles and puts a crease down the front of your retirement pants. Cash provides women, cars, places to live, beer money, and cigars—that's the dream. So, I save what I can from the money I earn as an independent debt collector and sometime hurt distributor.

I don't gotta tell you, work like mine can get complicated. Loan sharks and hustlers and grudge holders outsource more rigorous forms of persuasion to a guy like me so they can swear on their kids' eyes that they were somewhere else when bones got broke, heads got cracked, and money got got. Deniability is a key selling point for my services. That, and I'm willing to cross lines and back up threats with physical conviction. Call it a trait if you want: once committed to a goal, there ain't much that'll deviate my intention to get it done, especially if I'm getting paid.

There ain't a union protecting my rights, or a guaranteed minimum hourly rate wage for the service I provide. I get a set finder's fee for running debtors down who short their payments or let the vig on the principle run up beyond any possibility to square up. 10 percent of any monies recovered, and a negotiated fee for anything else the seeker of recompense needs me to do for them, is what I ask. I got a protective buffer that distances me from those contracting my skills: the separation of a middleman, who makes a strong case to those who engage my particular talents, that 10 percent, plus his cut, of the principle is better than 10 percent of nada.

When you boil it down, I'm not that different from 90% of the population who need to find a reliable income stream and then look for ways to distract themselves from the monotony of necessary employment that occupies 40 hours plus of every week of every month of every year until the lucky 1s get to retire and the unlucky 1s get dead.

What I do sounds intense when I admit to it out loud, even to me. But the job is largely scutwork—dull, drawn-out, methodical. It's rare that I gotta be more than 15 minutes bad in 1 day. When I'm staking out a potential bolt hole or scrolling through hours of social media trying to track someone's, or tracking someone who knows that someone's whereabouts, I fantasize *what-if* scenarios: what if I'd studied harder at school? – what if I'd learned a practical trade? – what if I'd got on the undercard of a title fight? – what if, what if, what ain't.

It can take weeks, sometimes months to get a lead, not always a successful lead, before a job becomes momentarily intense. I'm not squeamish about putting on the hurt, I've dealt out pain all my life, and, truth be told, I quite enjoy the vicious nature of what I do considering the type of degenerates I largely do it to.

I do draw the line at hurting kids—although, I'm not above kidnapping a defaulter's nearest and dearest to make a point. I ain't religious about keeping the faith, that would be unprofitable, but I loosely follow the code of a hand-me-down credo passed to me by a respected mentor in the business. A man who took me under his wing when I needed a fresh start and few questions asked. To be perfectly frank, most of the rules I try not to bend are survival tactics rather than pearls of wisdom that guide a disciple to felonious enlightenment.

I got no responsibilities outside of those I commit myself to. I don't own much in my name, and everything I do got I pay cash for. I got a comfortable ride... and that's about it. I live outta a carryall grip in moderately priced motels, so no fixed abode or ties to any belongings I can't throw in the trunk and take with. If you wanna contact me for work, you can't, unless you got my burner cell phone number, and the only person who has that is my go-between who gets their end up front from those who use our services before passing on the details to me. There are few friends in my social circle of acquaintances, and none of them so close that I'd miss their company if I never saw them again. I rub along with the regular Joes and Josephines I bump into and, for now, that's enough to not get lonely.

Outside of my go-between, I don't got any meaningful relationships to speak of, other than my brothers (who don't really like me much) and my sister and niece (who love me, even though I ain't around much—unless it's to remind her no-good ex that child support is due), and an old, well-kept, leather grip bag that 1st belonged to my old man. He died in 2013 of a non-hereditary form of progressive neurodegeneration called Dementia with Lewy Bodies. The disease is a fucked up vascular dementia that steals a sufferer's memory and physical functionality—a tragedy in a guy like my old man, whose bone-deep strength and bear claw hands are the only things of merit I inherited from him, other than his leather grip, that is. He was a hard worker, a plasterer by trade: early starts, late finishes, weekends, and he still had trouble making ends meet—a life lost that way is tragic. Anyway, he wouldn't have wanted to see his favorite scamp turn out like I did, so that's a small blessing, I suppose. My mother? She's a miserable cunt who could make Jesus take His own name in vain. The less said about that abusive, sacramental wino the better.

I may not field a 1st-pick career, but that don't mean I'm not on the bench for a 2nd-starter life. My long-term goal is to squirrel away sufficient fuck you bank and fuck off somewhere warm and stress-free. At some point I'll need to give my leather grip a rest from lugging around heavy tools, otherwise, my bag might end up in an evidence storage facility while I end up incarcerated for an extended period of my best years.

Thailand: where a little money stretches a long way; villa near the beach and a brown-skinned, STI-free, Thai wifey who can keep house, cook up traditional meals, make an effort to look good, and empty my balls on a regular basis, minus the kinda grief you'd get from 'wifeing' a woman with an American attitude—who really can't keep up basic niceties for long without fucking complaining or expecting a standing ovation anytime they do 1 thing for you. In the Good Ol' USofA, living the way I do, looking the way I do—like a thug—I attract a few women looking to spice up their lives with a dangerous fuck buddy, so I ain't celibate. I don't got an itch to get hitched or father any legit offspring or money-draining bastards, which is another reason my old man would've frowned upon my alternative lifestyle; he loved his kids—would've loved his granddaughter hard enough to break his heart if he hadn't croaked.

But I ain't retired yet, and that's why I'm currently working Las Vegas, tracking down an excessive wastrel owing an unforgiving loan shark 100Gs.

Having lost tabs on his debtor, this Detroit-based shylock contacted my contact about making contact with this deadbeat who keeps dodging payments on the vigorish let alone making good on the principle, outsourcing collection dues to me. If I can recover the principle, I get the juice. If the money's been dropped on the craps tables, then I get equivalent to the juice for breaking the delinquent's kneecaps. Either way, I'm expecting 10Gs for this 1—fair.

Naturally, fucking someone up who owes money so badly that they can't beg, borrow, or steal enough to settle accounts, is a stupid way of securing repayment. Even a few slaps can make things tough for a mark to rip off their workplace or sell their shit, unless it's on eBay, without awkward questions and suspicion about 'What the fuck happened to you?' No, the best way to get paid is with threat. A credible threat that you'll make the debtor or someone they care about pay 1 way or another if they ain't forthcoming with the cash or an acceptable solution.

It don't need to be physical harm you threaten a mark with: burn down their shed; smash gramma's 50-year-old garden gnome collection; steal their dog; slam a dirt torpedo into the hull of their jacuzzi. You break their hamster's legs, you slash the leather upholstery of their beloved ride, you find the right emotional trigger and you let them know that the only way the pain ends is after the debt's settled. 9 times outta 10 you can get almost anyone to cough up the cash or equivalent weight in valuables, even nana's under-the-mattress savings. If all else fails, you follow through on your threats or your reputation starts to sag like erectile dysfunction on a wedding night, and then the debt collection honeymoon's off.

Anyway, that's the stale roll of my history, the rest of this story's fresh out the oven. My past might pop up for context here and there, but it ain't necessary to tell the truth and shame the Devil about the sins I earned and won't atone for. What's done is done, and I couldn't do better because I am who I am. Even though I've said it, it goes without saying that I'm a hard man to know and a harder man to mess with.

# 2.

I'm on the clock, 10Gs ain't chicken feed, but my pay for this job comes outta the recovered cash, so I can't piss about for weeks on end chasing phantoms. I wouldn't even be here if my go-between hadn't got wind that our runner had run to Vagas for a seat in a backroom card game operating in the shadows thrown by the lights and fountains and glossy surfaces that showcase the glamorous façade of Sin City. Once I get over here, it's necessary to grease the palms of a few local guys who know their way around, and in 2 days I'd got a line on Jonathon Casey—the lowlife, pissant, gambling degenerate who shorted Detroit of big bills. 'Johny Moron' didn't even have the good sense to slip a thin end of the thick wedge he owed under his marker holder's door to keep civility open, so he's got it coming.

While I renew good relations with old informants, who ask around if anyone's sitting opposite the name I'm hunting, I get a room at the *Sandstone Inn*, a cash motel off the 'Strip', way off, with a pool, that don't look like it's swimming with Legionnaires Disease, and an ice machine, that don't look like it's been used to store dismembered body parts. History, the ice machine story, maybe I'll tell you about that some other time.

Yeah, I'm on the clock, but all work and no play make Saint a dull boy. So, I'm taking it easy on the motel bed, having just smashed the squeeze of this casino widow, the buxom Debbie, I'd flirted with a couple of times around the pool.

Debbie looks good sunbathing, a little plump in the thighs and butt, but she caught my eye lotioning her tanned skin in a 2 piece that showed me everything I wanted to know about her curves. Hubby's out with his buds losing at 1 of the casinos while I rod his wife's plumbing. The wife rocks up at my door after lunch in a shit ton of makeup, smokey eyeshadow and spider leg eyelashes, wearing an indecent minidress and high heel fuck me pumps, and holding a bottle of Jackie D in 1 hand, and a bottle of full-fat coke in the other.

"D'you wanna party?" she asks.

"Yeah, I'm in."

Call it a kink or a fetish, but I love trashy makeup on a trashy MILF, and better still when they're wearing it just for me.

What really turns me on, though, if I got the choice, is a cute-assed woman with an athletic bod who digs a masculine guy with a masculine attitude in the bedroom, 'cause I'm both, if you're into hard jawed faces, punch-thick noses, and scarred eyebrows. But hot chicks like that don't drop from the sky into your lap, I'm sorry to say, without running through the usual player pickup lines and throwing in a few adlibs to rev up the clichéd script. I can banter, but the gift of the gab ain't worth shit if a woman don't like the face the words are coming outta—and my face looks like trouble, whatever expression I pull it into.

Running down contracts all over the place, I don't generally got time to coax premium ass outta its panties. So, I set the hound on older, sometimes married, women who're gagging for a bit of rough to upend the mundane and take them from behind. It's a dominance thing, I think. Left on the shelf single women and mothers who've had to be self-reliant and independently strong, or married women with weak or absent husbands, get a timeout from being neglected or alone when they give it up to a powerful man. For some women, to be fucked because they're wanted by a man who'll treat them like a sexual object is halfway to a screaming orgasm. Having obligations and responsibilities set aside for a moment, or 2 moments if I'm feeling particularly energetic, is a break from reality for women whose reality is consistently real.

Take this guy Debbie's married to, he can't get away with the things I do to his wife. He wanted to come to Vegas on a boys' vacation, but she wouldn't let him without bringing her along to sip cocktails by the pool and sip another man's Johnson's in his room. If she caught hubby screwing around there'd be hell to pay, but sluts got double-standards when it comes to being slutty, and I got no problem with that.

Debbie and me don't got all day and night, the fun facet runs dry at 4 'cause I gotta be somewhere by 6, but we can get soaking wet until then. She's so desperate to abandon her morals, that she'll risk cheating on her regular life with an irregular man in a random motel room in the middle of the day when anyone around can see her propositioning me at my door—long live sexual liberation.

Having played out the fantasy in her mind, Debbie can't wait for me to make it come true, she's obviously spent a deal of time making herself as alluring as possible—my libido appreciates the work she's put in. She steps into my domain dressed in a figure-hugging blue minidress, painted nails, freshly shaved legs, and strappy heels.

Debbie's nervous. She barely knows me and knows nothing about my attitude in the bedroom. The lust in my eyes and pants is evident. She flutters her eyelashes. They say that the eyes are the windows to the soul: but in this case, they're the doorway to the bedroom. I presume that Debbie's infidelity is an indulgence rarely consummated, but I'm not the seducer, Debbie was seduced by the anticipation of being taken by a stranger. She's on vacation from the routine.

"Make yourself at home," I invite.

My room guest sashays her Junoesque butt over to the bed and pirouettes on her heels, "Do you have glasses?" she asks, holding up the bottles she brought with and batting her lashes like Egyptian Pharaoh fans.

I look her up and down, "Later," I say.

Shutting the room door, I take 3 steps to close the distance between us, pulling Debbie into me. My erection presses against the V of her dress when I kiss her on the mouth, flicking my tongue between her lips. My hands wander over her cinched-in waist, rounded hips, and ass. She throws the bottles on the bed, her hands mirror the enthusiasm of my exploring hands, they find my erection and tease it through my pants. Reservations are dropped quicker than a side alley whore's panties.

We get to know each other like that for a minute before Debbie unbuckles my belt and unbuttons my fly, dropping my pants and underwear to the floor, eager to fling herself into her fling. My dick springs free. She falls to her knees like a sinner before the pulpit. Flicking a snaking tongue, she blows me, the serpent tempts the spirit of Eve outta every woman's soul. To say that Debbie loves the taste of manhood, appreciates the male scent, relishes submission, that she responds to my hand on the back of her bottle-blonde head, wants the debasement of her femininity to take place in a cheap motel, is an understatement. She makes a meal of my prick like she ordered it off a 5-star menu. Her nail-polished hands grab my ass cheeks and pull me into her, 1 hand slipping 'round to caress my balls.

I wanna fuck her right away, but Debbie ain't eaten her fill, and I ain't feeding her a morsal. She's good. I gotta hold back from shortening the pleasure she's offering—I don't just wanna blowjob, I want all of her.

Blessed with thick thighs and an onion butt, I'm excited by every jiggle her dress fails to restrain. I throw my tee-shirt across the room, aiming for the desk chair, then I kick free of my pants legs and boxers, standing proudly naked. My fighter's physique and thuggish looks send a shiver of anxious anticipation through Debbie's opulent curves, held into form by a waist trainer corset and D-cup bra. We ain't here to flirt, conversational foreplay was made 'round the pool, we're here to fuck convention, fuck the vows of marriage, and to fuck. So, I snap on a rubber while she wriggles outta her dress so we can get down to business.

A margin note for anyone raw-dogging stray bitches like a dog: I spend a lot of my days trying not to get injured or dead, why would I risk dick gangrene plunging some unknown P and A when I can roll on protection, and then roll it off again when I'm done humping the sack?

On the bed we kiss, the incongruity of hard maleness against her soft femineity stiffens my erection ready for penetration. Debbie shimmies outta her panties while I collect the bottle of 'Black Label' and coke off the bed. Unscrewing the whiskey cap, I give Debbie a neat swig from the neck and then take a warm burn myself. She stalks like a panther to the edge of the mattress and sticks her ass in the air. It's peachy round and angrily red on 1 side where I slap it. I kiss the welt, nibble down with my teeth, and bite her inner thigh, just hard enough to make her squeal with shocked delight.

When I push in, Debbie moans like I'm filling a deep emptiness. I reach around and pet the cat, Debbie's gasping breath as rapid as a rabbit's heartbeat. When I get full inside, she pushes back against me, taking all I got to offer. I unhook her bra and overhand lob it somewhere in the vicinity of her panties, and then set up a cheek-clapping rhythm, inserting deep and slow, building to a pumping chorus of pleasure that spills from her glossy mouth in ecstatic groans. Ripples clap with every thrust. I grip Debbie's hips to pull myself into her, her own hand taking the place of mine so I can concentrate my efforts on sexual endurance.

The mutual rhythm of bumping uglies builds. Our instinct to please and take pleasure ain't premeditated, there wasn't agreement beforehand that I'd take her from behind, the attitude we discover comes naturally. Hard and fast and faster, burying her face into the pillow, her muffled cries of satisfaction are orgasmic.

My tempo and depth and angle are postured to please us both—I'm not overly charitable when it comes to single-use women like Debbie, but there's a certain amount of gratification in being the man who gets them off. Her blissful whimpers rise to climax, I drill down into the core of her pleasure, penetrating so deep that, in an ecstatic moment of release, I touch her soul.

"Oh yeah, I'm sooo close, keep fucking me!" she insists.

"Fuck yeah, I'm coming with," I give notice of an imminent emptying of my balls.

That stimulates Debbie into sexual convulsions. She encourages rough passion. I pound her Pilates tight pelvic floor with an urgency that slams the headboard into the wall. Slamming her into complete surrender, she cries out loud enough to inform the room occupants either side that we're nearly done thrashing out a frantic finish.

"Cum for me, Daddy!"

WTF, Debbie's just about old enough to be my mommy, but there's no stopping me now. I cum, loudly and fully. Wanting the absolute feeling of release to go on forever, but the sensory override is too potent to hold onto, and I only have so much fluid to give. With my balls and enthusiasm drained by the tight center of Debbie's pussy, I enter that euphoric lightness you get when the thought of sex and the act of sex drops in the order of importance. The wife whose marriage vows I just violated no longer holds the same hounding appeal, so I give her butt a final slap that'll leave a handprint she'll have to hide from her husband for an hour or two.

Debbie yelps. Collapses on the bed and rolls over, her huge tits artfully drape across her panting ribcage, "That was nice."

"Another drink?"

"Sure, then we can fuck again."

"I gotta be somewhere."

"Shame."

"Debbie, you're an awesome ride," I kiss her on the mouth, tender this time, just to show how much I appreciate the offer.

5 minutes later, Debbie's in the bathroom removing smudged makeup from her face and showering off the stink of me. I'm lying out on the bed, sipping neat JD, with a deck of cigarettes on my lap, another bad habit I can't seem to shake, although, the urge to smoke generally takes me only after sex, after a few drinks, or after a near miss.

One of my cell phones rings—I got 3: 1 for personal banking and only that (secured in the room safe along with my wallet and anything else I wanted... safe), 1 for personal-personal, used for keeping in touch with those outside the life, and 1 for work (the work cell is a burner phone that gets swapped out at the end of any job that involves arrestable circumstances)—it's the ringtone for work chiming.

I pick it up, hold it to my ear, and answer with a smoky, "Yeah?"

"Halo, it's, Duke," a gruff voice confirms that the caller is 1 of the few people who has this number; "Can you talk?"

I don't keep an extended contacts list writ down or stored on any device, that information is hidden in the digital cloud at the end of a password rainbow. There're times I need to store a contact for a few weeks that I ain't gonna memorize so I type it in, and I got Duke's matching burner logged. Other than that, I mostly meet and greet contacts face-to-face. Whenever I use my work cell, I delete the call log after the conversation's done. I don't use biometric recognition on any device. All my passwords are in my head. No 1 can get into my business or personal info without an unsmiling effort at changing my opinion about what's the least painful option for me—the option of giving an interrogator what they want or forcing them to try and take it from me. That way I'm only 1 bad concussion away from becoming a man with 3 cells and no 1 I can remember to call.

"Give me a sec," I stall, glancing at the bathroom door, where the sounds of running water and a buxom, completely satisfied, HRT-stacked 50-year-old singing like a soprano is emanating.

With the phone on the bed, I quickly dress in enough clothes to not get arrested for public indecency when I go and take the call outside. I leave my shoes and socks and underwear on the chair and slide the room key into my front pocket, with a deck of smokes and cheap gas lighter in my back in the event of a 2-smoke conversation.

"Hey," I shout through the bathroom door; "I'm just outside taking a work call," I let Debbie know.

"OK," a muted response, still at a soprano pitch, calls back.

Outside in bare feet, I'm free to talk, albeit in euphemisms and roundabout language, a precaution that me and my go-between worked out as an extra layer of confusion—just in case. At this time of day, guests and motel staff are back and forth from the pool and rooms and office and Vagas Strip, so it's wise to be indirect.

"Halo, you mixing work with pleasure? Getting down and dirty with a Vagas pro?"

"Nah, it's a wife-jacking. I ain't paying for nothing an amateur's giving away free."

"Ha, I hear that. What happens in..."

"...yeah, yeah, Vagas stays in Vagas," I cut my contract negotiator off; "What d'you want, Duke?"

"How close are you to finding our neighbor and getting our lawnmower back?"

Duke and me have known each other long enough that we use a shorthand code when we're speaking on the phone or emailing each other, even when we consider the device secure. 'Lawnmower', for instance, means the green stuff some defaulter borrowed and ain't returned—it's a take on the stereotypical sitcom neighbor who borrows all the tools from the main character's garage and never brings them back, only a cuntier version. 'Neighbor' means the mark – 'Needs a hammer' is cryptic slang for a neighbor who's due a beating – 'Crowbar' means repo a neighbor's shit or his place – 'Clamp it down' means put the squeeze on – 'Loan our neighbor a box of nails' means fitting some poor son of a bitch for a coffin. Anyway, you get the idea, if anyone overhears us talking shop, the meaning behind what the fuck we're saying has to be proved rather than recounted as a verbatim transcript of criminal intent—it's basic 'Yada-yada', 'Forget about it' argot.

I flick my first and deal myself a second Maverick from the deck and light up. I draw a post-coitus lungful and blow a smokey answer into the mic, "Just waiting for word from a sub-contractor (informant). Seems our neighbor's moving from 1 house to another, but he's ordered up a special delivery for tonight and my Vegas guy's running down an address for us. I think the problem needs a clamp to fix it."

"Whatever gets the mower back in good order. But that ain't what I'm calling about."

"Oh, yeah?"

"A neighbor of ours (client) has a ride-on mower (a shit ton of green) gone missing and needs it back to finish their lawn... interested in picking it up and driving it back?"

"What's the gas tank on a machine like that?"

"4000-liters ($4-million = 400-liter commission)."

Our mobile network connection mutes into absolute silence while I do the math. 400-liters would siphon a cool 400l into my tank, boosting my retirement reserve to 550l, leaving 50-liters running around gas. Of course, that quantity of compostable trimmings is likely to turn into a compost of rotting vegetation—dirty green stinks until you wash it.

"We should meet," my rational mind gets dry-mouthed at the reward vs. risk of a commission on this scale, but my reckless side is positively drooling over the whiff of all that odorous moolah.

"Agreed, Half 'n Half?"

"I'll be there tomorrow 'round midday."

"Drive safe, Halo."

"Later, Duke."

# 3.

For what it is, The *Sunny V Motel* off the Main Strip—not as removed as my motel is from Las Vegas Boulevard—is a moderately respectable motel that still accepts cash. And what it is, is somewhere Jonathon Casey is holed up between throwing good money after bad and betting on changing his luck in 1 of the backroom card games that the knaves of Vagas run for the kings of dubious enterprise. I leave my current runaround—a 2020 blue Kia Soul—in the parking lot of a 24-hour diner catering for 24-hour people with 24-hour appetites, preferring to walk up to the motel so I can scout it out. It's your typical 2-story place: ground-floor rooms open onto the parking lot, with cement stair access from the pavement up to a 1st-floor balustraded walkaround.

It's 9pm, the sun has dropped from the scene, and the Main Strip is drawing thousands of Vegas moths to its light, turning the dull peripheral side streets into vague throughways.

Carrying my leather work grip in my left hand, leaving my right hook free in case I needed to swing, I dodge the illumination thrown by a pink and green stilt sign announcing the motel's name and vacancies, skirting the parking lot shadows. If you don't scrutinize too hard, I'm a guest dressed on the unassuming side of casual heading for his room. Dark, loose-fit clothing, plain black baseball cap, soft-soled black shoes, and black leather gloves with touch-screen fingertips. If you do take notice, then I look like a tooled-up, 215lbs housebreaker on the prowl—risk, it's part of the job, you gotta wear it or change your occupation and clothing.

Casey has a room booked for a week. The room number I've been given is 21, ironic considering the age of his special delivery. In the parking space allocated to room 21 sits a used, faded silver Audi. Last I heard, Casey was driving a much newer model. Sticking to the same car make, as Audi cunts tend to, he must have traded-in the newer cuntmobile he drove to Vagas for a cheaper model, using the cash he got in part-exchange for his stake. I dismiss the car, it ain't an asset worth taking, not that I consider Audi's assets in any condition, but I might've been able to offload it onto some other tasteless *fotze* or a cash chop shop if it was in better condition.

I time my crossing while the route is clear, climbing the stairs before some civilian decides to get ice from the communal box near a deuce of snack vending machines on the ground floor. Even at this late hour, I'm wearing shades, precautionary face-furniture obscuring my features on any security cameras—I reach the 1st-floor landing without tripping up the steps in the polarized twilight.

When my Vagas guy gave up Casey's whereabouts, he also got me a master key for the motel that bypasses the swipe. Why, where, who, and how he came into possession of this information, and an actual room key, is between him and his sources, and the reason I filled my Vagas guy's tank with gas.

I give the window a side-eye when I pass the room.

Nothing.

The drapes are pulled tighter than Debbie's Pilates squeeze, and the TV's turned up loud to hide any telltale noises coming from inside. I'd taken the liberty of lubing the key with a dab of 3in1 oil, so it slides into the lock and turns without a hitch. I'm inside with the door closed behind me quicker than a striking cobra with a Tourettes tic.

A fully-naked bald guy, with a receding hairline that's practically neck hair, a shallow soft-muscled chest, and a face like a Spud-U-Don't-Like potato jumps up from the bed, upending the girl he'd been molesting onto the floor.

*"Sit the fuck down, Casey!"* I warn, something in my voice persuades him to drop back onto the mattress edge, I don't need to pull a heater.

Casey gives me a fuckwit squint with weepy, myopic eyes. He doesn't know who I am, but he can guess why I'm here. We ain't got to the bare bones of how our transaction is gonna stew—boiling fast or simmering long—but I'm setting the temperature of our unscheduled appointment to hot.

I note his prescription glasses on the nightstand, and that his erection has toppled like a Jenga tower. He covers the offending organ in the cup of both hands—he only needs 1 for the unimpressive crotch needle he's got in his sewing kit. With or without his designer glasses, which he undoubtedly believes are white-framed cool as fuck, he's the spit of a classic pedophile next-door mugshot. If this fucker lived next door to me, he'd stay the fuck away from peeping on me from his windows or I'd smash all the panes and make him eat glass until he shit his insides out. Just his ugly scumbag mug inspires violent communication, and that's a bad beginning for someone I'm gonna siphon 120-liters outta.

The girl rolls over on the carpet. She's very naked and very young. The makeup obscuring her youthful features looks absurd; her ginger hair's styled from an era long before she was born; her small breasts are just in bud; her knock-knee thighs and tomboy butt ain't filled in yet; and her pubic-V is downy. I put her age around 13 or 14—Johnny 'Chomo' Casey is a deviant piece of shit at the tables and in the bedroom.

"Give the girl a bed sheet," I order her abuser.

Casey does as he's told. He's already compliant. He won't need much convincing to give me want I want, but sometimes a violent attitude in the face of weakness is hard to contain, especially if you're committed to making the other guy pay.

"Get your things and go wait in the bathroom," I tell the girl, who promptly wraps her tiny midriff in the sheet and collects her white heels, blue denim miniskirt, a pink boob-tube, and a tiny shoulder bag—probably full of condoms and a little speed—from the chair. Her eyes are hazel and wide and scared, her pupils drugged into dilation; "Go ahead, get dressed. Better leave your cell phone on the dresser," I advise.

I don't need a recording catching me out or a 911 call inviting the cops to the party.

She does as asked, takes the cell from her bag and places it on the dresser. Closing the bathroom door when she leaves me to my business. I hear the lock click. The TV's loud enough that I can't hear if she's crying in there, but most regular civilians do, even those connected to the life get jumpy when I swing by looking like the gorilla you stole a banana from.

"Look..."

*"Shut the fuck up!"* I ain't playing, I ain't negotiating, I ain't listening to any piss poor excuses, that ain't my style; "I'll do the asking and you do the answering. Every time you open your mouth to crap out some bullshit I didn't ask for, I'm gonna take a tooth. D'you got me?" I use a street-tough vernacular, a way of talking I've picked up like a foreign accent that creeps into an ex-pat's voice from speaking another language for a long while. Even to me, I sound like a scripted movie gangster sometimes, but the tone has an edge to it that makes it real.

Casey nods and gulps out a, "Yeah."

I take off my sunglasses and slip them into my back pocket. Then I put my heavy grip bag on the luggage stand and lean my back into the wall facing the crumpled bed.

Casey's cell's on the nightstand. I can't see any weapons. I'm physically and psychologically stronger than this piss-poor excuse for a human being—I ain't worried.

"D'you know who I am?"

Casey shakes his head.

I look meaningfully at my bag, then back at him, "I go by Halo."

This time he nods, and the fear I'd seen in the girl's eyes doubles in his, "You're the saint against sinners."

"Something like that. You know why I'm here?"

"The money."

"Right, the money. I'm here to collect."

"I…"

"…is this something I wanna hear?"

He shakes his head.

"Don't fucking test me, you child-raping cunt, or you'll find out what's in the fucking bag."

In the life, you regularly have professional affiliations with the bad men of this world. Some affiliations I'd made are even what you might consider friendly, and 1 close friend of mine was a mentor for the collection business. 7 years ago, when I found out that there was an assault and battery case building against me, a case likely to send me down for a stretch, 'Big Bob' Crookston, a twice-convicted felon working on his 3rd strike, commiserated about my upcoming trail and likely sentence but consoled that I'd get to tax all the child molesters I'd come across inside if I couldn't tax lowlifes like Casey on the outside.

Big Bob's favorite pastime when he was stretching time, was to find bad paperwork on a chomo and take out his rage and twisted sense of justice on these miserable reprobates—"*They got it coming,*" he'd preach like a puritanical inquisitor on Torquemada's God squad. He even had a prison ink tally needled into his forearm like a badge of honor for every kiddy-diddler he put in the infirmary. I didn't have any prison ink, and I didn't wanna compensate my loss of freedom by lashing out at other inmates and having my sentence extended—not when I can do it on the outside and get paid to fuck them up—so I kept my nose clean(ish) and did my time.

I walk over to the closet and slide the door back, bolted to the wall inside is a room safe with keypad access.

"Give me the combination. Sit on your hands while I key it in. Don't fucking move or I'll snap your neck and get answers outta your paralyzed ass," I don't want him making for the door while I'm distracted.

Casey removes his cupped hands from his shriveled prick and balls and sits on them, "452..." Beep, Beep, Beep, "823..." Beep, Beep, Beep, "283#B." Beep, Beep, Beep, Beep.

The safe lets out a correct beep alert and the keypad LED turns from red to green popping the internal bolt allowing the lock mechanism to twist and the door to swing.

"Alright, what have we got here?"

Casey watches my every move from the mattress, his hands under his butt, his prick a tiny miserable-looking anemic slug in his lap.

I check inside the safe. A stack of cash, a Rolex that would need another bracelet link to fit me, a couple of gold rings I can pawn to pay for the watch alteration with money left over for gas, and a Kimber Micro 9 KHX pocket pistol with a snakeskin grip design. It's a nice gun. The magazine holds 7 9mm rounds. I check the mag, clip it back, check the safety, but don't rachet a round into the chamber. I don't wanna accidental discharge cutting a new cleft in my ass when I slide it under my waistband at the back next to my own heater. If this was my room, I'd keep the gun close by, probably snuggled beside the Gideon Bible in the nightstand drawer. Maybe Casey's worried the girl would get hold of the weapon and put a bullet between his balls after he did what he planned to do to her and that's why his piece is locked away?

As a precaution, I'd service the weapon later, using gloves so that none of my fingerprints would be on the internal mechanism, cartridges, or ejected mag. Everything else in the safe I lay out on the dresser. A quick estimate of the cash comes to 20-liters and some drip—my end.

"Looks like you're doing OK?" I inventory, speculating that Casey has been involved in a few backroom poker games as you don't come out in front playing at the casino tables.

By all accounts, this guy can't help himself when it comes to gambling. If 2 gulls take a midair dump, he'd bet on which squit will splatter the sidewalk 1st.

"Right. Now the cell phone."

"What?"

"Don't make me repeat myself."

He releases his right hand and reaches for the cell, swiping the face and tapping out the security code. Like me, Casey don't rely on biometric ID to access his sensitive data. An unconscious fingerprint is just as recognizable as a conscious 1; a face with a slapped cheek is just as identifiable as an unslapped 1.

In the movies, the 1st pain an enforcer inflicts when he wants to get someone to talk is to the face. You don't get coherent replies from someone you need to break when they're strapped to a chair getting punched hard enough to fracture eye sockets, bust lips, loosen teeth, burst blood vessels, blacken eyes, knock them the fuck out—have you ever tried to make sense of someone taking with a fractured jaw?

No. Serious professionals, and I acknowledge that there are plenty of psychopaths and fuckwits in my line that we shouldn't include in this statement, employ tactics of intimidation, coercion, and non-invasive persuasion to get results. If we do gotta work a guy over, then we start at the feet and work our way up, only disfiguring the identifiable parts of his or her anatomy if we need to conceal the identity of someone we've worked to death. It'd be like slashing all the tires on your only ride when the treads are worn and then trying to drive to the tire depot on flats, it makes no fucking sense.

I take the cell from Casey's outstretched hand, keeping my distance so he don't try something desperate. Swiping through the apps, I find his online banking link, then get him to cough up the codes—50 grand. He's short by 1/2 what he owes my current employer, and fuck knows how much is due to any other sharks he's baited for capital. But everyone else he owes will have to get in line, I'm collecting 1st.

I transfer what there is into an escrow holding account that my employer and Duke can access through the worldwide wonder of the interweb, and then throw the cell onto the dresser along with his personal shit.

"Is there any more?"

"Can I speak?" he pleads in a weasel tone.

"Go ahead... but make it quick."

"Look, I've got a seat at a heavy game tomorrow. If you let me keep the cash, I can triple it, easy. With the 50 you cleaned outta my account that'll cover what I owe and I'll cut you in for a bigger slice of the action, right?"

"It won't cover the juice."

"In a week, I can get it all."

"Don't be stupid, Casey. In a week you'll still be on crutches."

"What?"

# 4.

The 1 stop motel, diner, bar, and gas station is as good as many and better than most places to sleep, to eat, to drink, to fill up with gas, and to meet up.

Duke and me came across the *Halfway Inn's* merits while toing and froing across the Midwest chasing down cash debtors and those owing broken limbs to the big boys affiliated with 1 organization (and I use that term loosely in some cases) or another. Duke's free-weights big, but he ain't a pitbull like me. His ears ain't cuffed into cauliflowers and his nose don't snort in his sleep from taking a snapping left-hook in the ring. He's never really experienced desperate pain or exhaustion and don't got the stomach to inflict more brutality on another human being than a pistol-whipping. His scars are scuffed knees and emotional trauma rather than split eyebrows and physical damage.

Duke runs his own jobs as well as mine to make dough, but the serious meat on his table he serves up for me to carve. Knives, hammers, hatchets, machetes, and pliers are strictly for the tool shed, the garage, or the kitchen as far as my go-between's concerned. I've never hanged a picture or cut down a tree, though, I hanged a man from a tree once, so hammers and rope are domestic tools conscripted into weapons of torture and war for me. Not that I don't like guns, I'd appropriated Casey's pocket pistol for just in case, and I keep a clean .45 stowed under the Kia's driver's seat, but guns equal spent cartridges and a loss of earnings. I point a gun at someone and all I'm collecting is their filthy soul.

Before I got pinched, Duke and me rubbed shoulders working the clubs and bars around Illinois, Peoria, and then around Chicago, we even trained at a weights gym together from time to time and kinda got to depend on each other when things got tight.

Duke fell into debt collection as a sideline. He knew steroid dealers who knew suppliers who knew the rackets that would pay under-the-table money for under-the-radar work. I helped out for pocket money, found I got a talent for inspiring quick results, and that talent introduced me to Big Bob. When my life and career got flushed, Duke gave me a wedge from his own putback to set me up after I was released from jail, and Bob partnered me 50/50 rather than as a backup man.

I paid Duke back in full, with a little sweetener on top as soon as—being indebted to someone, even a buddy, don't sit well.

Bob, well Bob got his 3rd strike beating up a hooker and her pimp and their dope dealer in a cocaine frenzy that would've scared the shit outta me had I been there. 2 cops showed up. Big Bob made them regret graduating from the police academy, and then the riot squad came in hot with beanbag rounds and tasers, introducing Bob to the nearest ER medical professionals who treated him for battered external soft tissues and bruised internal organs, severe concussion, and a massive cocaine come down. The judge was in no way amused by the fracas and sent my mentor down for 20, taking a hard man off the streets and probably saving a couple of 100 kneecaps from being broken—he'll be 80 by the time he's eligible for parole.

When I'm at a loose end, I sometimes make time to visit Bob at Stateville Correctional Center and shoot the shit for a minute. And every time I thicken my wedge of green using the knowledge he passed onto me, I bump his commissary with a $100 credit. It's the least I can do, working alongside Big Bob solidified my rep for following through on collections, making me a sought-after repossession man.

I don't got no dependents, though I have set up a trust fund for my niece with a starter bump in it for college and sundries—sentimental, I guess. I might get a few big commissions throughout the year, but that don't mean I can pass on the nickel-and-dime work that keeps the gas tank filled. You can't be picky about who you do work for or when or how much when you're close to running on empty—I don't like dipping into my retirement fund, that money's a shrine to the future. Here and there I swerve a job, but I ain't never turned down a collection that tops 5-litres. I've even collected from some backstory motherfuckers who'd given me a hard time when they had the upper hand—yeah, a bit of vindictive payback feels almost as good as getting backpay.

Although most of the work coming my way is through Illinois, the debtors I trace tend to have opted out of the state to avoid OG taxation, so I pick up the tab for those who can't afford to delegate work like this to the enforcers on their own crews engaged in regular hustles—losing money to chase money is a counterproductive move. So, I'm an outsourced resource, employed by bad men to do bad things on their behalf.

What else am I gonna do? Cash is king and I get sick just thinking about what it takes to earn a living wage paycheck. However tough I think I am, I ain't so tough that I can tough out a 9-to-5 job. Our thing is more a case of who you know rather than what you know. There are plenty of dumbasses in our business to deal with, but stupidity is a money-making enterprise for debt collectors who know the right people who loan cash to the wrong people to ride the money-go-round. Fortunately, Duke's a natural at picking up contacts and contracts. Me? I'm the blunt force trauma element of our crew. A 2-man crew that's lasted beyond my transition from saint to sinner and provides bona fides in the underground boom or busted money markets.

As associates, Duke and me know a lot of the crimes committed by each other. We're pretty close, but that don't mean I blab about the heinous details of an indictable aftermath to him. If 1 of us goes state's evidence and sells out the other for a get-outta-jail-free card or reduced sentence, my partner'd have more bargaining chips than me to buy himself outta trouble. Honor amongst thieves... bullshit. The criminal underworld is a horde of rats looking to avoid the traps and steal the cheese. Some rats are more verminous than others. The idea that we live by a code of silence, which is true to a greater or lesser extent when it comes to the Feds, drops from a 10th-floor balcony and smashes into a bloody pulp when there's a scary motherfucker with a leather grip bag full of Home Depot implements threatening to recondition the interior design of your body into a heap of exterior debris.

Me, in my mind, I'd rather intimidate the witnesses and garrote any snitches on the CI books than give up the 411. Still, I won't say I'd *never* consider a serious WITSEC offer dangled like a golden carrot for dropping another lowlife in the hole to keep me outta 1—but I wouldn't drop 1 of my own. Duke's a straight shooter and not a backstabber, so it would take a lot for me to give him up without cattle prod to the testicle's encouragement, and I trusted his balls would hold out just as long for me. I'd take a beating, take the heat myself, rather than rat him out. All the same, what he don't know can't hurt me. My un-inclusive retirement plan is 1 such secret I ain't sharing with anyone but myself. But yeah, him and me are close.

The *Halfway Inn* and attached diner face the highway. Motel rooms run either side of the rectangular structure, with an additional wing, where the office is at, making a right angle next to the gas pumps.

I pull the Kia into a spot for diner patrons and go in. Duke's waiting in a window booth looking out on the lot where we can keep an eye on our respective rides. The place is busy, not overcrowded, but a snapshot through the window would inform passersby that this is a good-eating establishment. Me and Duke will be speaking in tongues when discussing business, so the non-disciples of crime won't be tuned into our conversation, but we ain't gonna broadcast any specifics above volume 3, anyhow.

"Duke."

"Halo."

We greet.

I slip into the booth facing my partner. I hadn't eaten for a while. Duke's got a half-eaten bacon cheeseburger and fries in front of him. I was gonna get in on that action, so I get the waitress' attention. A neat blonde in a dark blue uniform and happy to help light blue eyes waits our booth.

"I'll have the same as my friend, and a Dr Pepper."

She makes a note in her order pad, "Coming right up," I'm assured.

"You get your wages OK?" I ask.

I know the transfer went through to the account Duke set up for the last job, but I ask anyway.

"Yeah, I got my 5. Filled the client's tank with 45. He was still pissed about the outstanding, so we might have to find our neighbor again in a couple of months and tax him for the rest."

"About that. I oughta give it a year, at least."

"Oh, yeah?"

"The guy had a work accident and won't be onsite for a while."

Offsite permanent implies that the accident was fatal, so Duke knows our guy is worse for wear but alive.

"Bad, was it?"

"He won't be walking it off anytime soon."

After I'd taxed Casey, the degenerate pedo motherfucker, on all the ready funds I can lay my hands on, I lay my hands on him as a tax on his predilection for child rape—you abuse a kid, any kid, and you abuse every father, mother, aunt, and uncle who loves and protects their own; and some uncles get pissed when an unprotected kid gets passed around like they're a plaything.

Duct-taping his disgustingly soft, lily-white torso to the room's desk chair, I tape his ankles to the chair legs, leaving his balls in his lap. His prick has shriveled so small that it looks like an outie bellybutton. I find his pants and whip the belt through the loops, not to beat him with it, but to curb the screams he's about to make. I move my grip to the bed and rummage through, choosing a ball-peen hammer as the method I'll apply arbitrary taxation.

"No, no, no, no, no don't do it. Don't do it, please. I'll get the money, I can get it all, you don't have to do this..."

"This is happening, Casey, don't waste your breath. But this ain't for stiffing the big boys you borrowed money from. I'm gonna fuck you up for stiffing kids. You got it coming. You don't gotta take it like a man, but you're gonna take it. Now bite down on this."

I stuff his belt between his teeth and then commenced *eeny, meeny, miny, moeing* his toes to the hammerhead beat of that nursery rhyme. The piece of shit actually voids his bowel, stinking up the room as tears run down his ugly mug, mixing with loosened snot. By the time I'd crunched my way across 10 toenails rather than wood nails, there's blood, piss, shit, snot, tears, and sobs leaking outta the fucker like butt clap gonorrhea.

I cover the shaking douchebag with a sheet from the closet and let his victim outta the bathroom. She's been crying. Probably thinks it's her turn to touch pain after hearing the drumbeat of violent hammering. She don't dare look at the sobbing ghost sitting in the corner of the room. From the gas money, I separate 4-liters and press it into her trembling hand.

I give her cell phone back with 2 requests, "Don't call no cops, d'you hear?" she nods; "Use the money to get yourself outta this life. You get fucked this young, you stay fucked. Take it from me, you can't get clean living in a dirty world."

She nods, again, she leaves. Whether she'll follow my advice or go on a teenage bender with her payoff, who knows? But I gotta give kudos to Big Bob's attitude towards chomos, I did feel a lot better about life after I'd minced Casey's feet into a pint of toe jam.

From inside the motel room, even above the TV volume and the blubs of a whimpering cunt, I can hear the child prostitute's ridiculous heels clip-clopping at a run along the 1st-floor walkway—if she was my niece, her abuser would be dead. By the time her shoes hit the pavement, I'm outta the room myself, covering my features so I won't get caught in 4K. I take Casey's watch and jewelry to pawn, take his cell phone and trash it with the bloody hammer, and then pull out the wires connecting the room's internal phone. Last of all, I kick Casey's chair over. Unless 1 of his neighbors are willing to get involved with a police investigation, the child-abusing son of a bitch will have to make enough noise that someone from reception will come up to check out the commotion before he can get medical attention.

On the drive outta Vegas, I stop at a pawnbroker to sell the jewelry and get the Rolex bracelet resized. It's such a common thing that the broker don't ask for provenance, thinking I'm just another Sin City punter punching outta Nevada with a little road money and a new watch.

"Forget about it," I give Duke the timeworn wiseguy response for a foozled situation.

"Fair," he agrees.

"OK, sell me the pitch."

Duke takes a sip of his cola and smiles, that's a bad sign, "It's heavy, but so are the risks. If you wanna skip under the ropes, I get it, but wait 'till you hear the 1st bell before deciding if you're gonna lace up your gloves or not," he warns, leaning in on his elbows so that his jacket creaks like a leather easy chair being crushed by a hard-assed 240lb bodybuilder.

I spin a finger in a 'Let's wind the long intro on' motion, "A 4000-liter machine's gonna have a lot of torque," I bring up.

"The mower's in St. Louis. I don't think it's gonna be a quick rake to bag the clippings, more like a wait for the right weather before mowing the lawn deal."

"I don't know St. Louis too well."

"I gotta name who knows the layout over there but doesn't have the know-how to mow the lawn."

A 'name' ain't a 'guy', a 'name' is an unknown guy we're trusting on spec, possibly vouched for, but certainly not 1 of our proven guys. I give my chin a good rub, thinking about what's on the table and what's alluded to. Then the waitress returns to place my food on an actual table.

"Can I get you anything else?"

"Nah, I'm good, thanks… Duke?"

"I'm fine."

"OK. Just holler if you need me. Enjoy."

Our waitress leaves with a good service smile on her lips, or so I think.

"She's zeroed you, Halo."

"Who… the waitress?"

"Man, any more obvious and she'd be offering herself on the menu."

"I hadn't noticed," I admit, looking over at her servicing another table, where we catch each other's eye; "Too hungry to notice, I guess," I rationalize my lapse of awareness, taking a gator-sized bite of my burger.

"Too much Vagas pussy more like. You done worn yourself out," Duke laughs.

I laugh along with, "Something like that," I admit without admitting details.

"So, what d'you think?"

"About the waitress or the job?"

"Whether you give the waitress a large tip or not is your business. Setting up this job is mine."

"I could take a trip and spec the work, see if it's doable? I'd have'ta hear more about it first."

"Fair. I got you a new cell. You still got that cover ID?"

"Yeah, I got a cover ID I can use."

I'd cut a flap in the underside of Kia's spare tire and stuffed a bag inside with some emergency cash and my IDs, packed it tight so it wouldn't rattle, and then dabbed the flap closed with some superglue. You'd have to lift the spare outta the wheel well and spot the flap to know what I'd done. To get at my hidden stash, I'd jimmy it open with a knife, replace my legal legend with a fake ID and stick the rubber back before sticking the spare in the trunk for safekeeping. If I get a flat, I got a canister of tire repair foam that'd get me to the nearest garage, so it's a practical hack—Duke don't know about it.

"We'll discuss the details in the lot... when you've finished your burger," he suggests guardedly, sipping his drink, and waiting for me to top up my calories.

# 5.

Route 44 is a straight run at St. Louis. The drive from Cherokee Nation takes 6 hours. I'd have made it in under 5 if I hadn't stopped at *Dickey's Barbeque Pit* for a Rib Combo, and then at *Lowe's Home Improvement* to replace the duct tape I'd used strapping Casey to an ad hoc chiropodist chair so I could work on his feet. It took 10 minutes gutting my spare to retrieve the ID I'd be using, my other life got pushed into the rubber void, and the hole sealed with glue—it would sit in the tire well for the duration.

I drive the Kia within speed limits, giving way when I got to, keeping road rage to myself; mirror, signal, maneuvering like a driver's ed A student. I fly under the radar, in a speed trap sense of the expression as well as a not drawing attention to myself sense.

With the new burner phone, I finalized journey details in the *Halfway Inn* parking lot, planning my route and stops via Google Maps. My personal cell phones are shut down before starting out, I don't want a signal trail pinging every cell tower along the highway to where I'll be lodging. I'll be paying my way in cash too. I only use a credit card or digital wallet when I got to: digital spoor is a spreadsheet of activity that some keyboard tracker in a cozy office can pick up and follow without wearing out their shoe treads, so I exercise caution whenever possible.

"You're not driving that piece of shit Kia to St. Louis, are you?" Duke asks leaning against a '23 cobalt blue Mazda CX-5.

"I like it. It ain't got drift or drag but it's got some street hustle, don't stand out, and it's registered under an alias."

"Shit, come on, Halo, it ain't gangster and you're a fucking OG."

We can talk freely outside, the euphemisms drop like spent cigarette butts.

"Duke, you like flash cars more than wet pussy."

"I need both, it's an addiction this next job's gonna help support."

"Tell me about it."

"There's this connected guy, Riccardo Caduto, in St. Louis who's running a small casino as a dirty money laundry for a syndicate outta Chicago. He's got some muscle to keep the locals honest, the legit setup's profitable, but the skim's short. A cool 4-mil short they estimate, so someone's skimming the skim and the big boys ain't too pleased about it. Anyway, this guy they got managing the place has a handler who's on the books. Everyone expects a little side action from a hustler, but the handler ain't declaring nothing, so the management's sus.

It's SpaghettiOs and ketchup: you can't separate the sauce from the sauce. And no 1 knows who's loyal to who, who else might be getting a taste, who's protecting what and who and why, so straight-out accusation could whip up a shitstorm. Our backer's decided outsourcing's the way to go.

He's used us before for out-a-state jobs, so we're known."

"This is sketch. The whole thing sounds... complicated... shot in the head complicated. How am I 'sposed to lean on a syndicate handler and connected casino manager and make them bend? I ain't that heavy, and I ain't Danny 'Fuck the Mob' Greene neither," that, plus I was kinda done with casinos and gambling after spending 4 days in Bling Vagas with the degenerates and pervs. The thought of playing hot potato with the pinky ring mob didn't inspire.

"Hear me out before you take a swerve on this 1. We got a St. Louis guy already on the inside and he can get you in as an associate, right. So, you go, do a few lowkey jobs for the management, and get paid for scoping the mark. Chicago's fronting us 10Gs each to take a look-see. If the manager's rinsing the mob's laundry into his own washer, then you got a green light to get it back and then disappear him if you find a way to do it without throwing shade on our backer. If you can't, report back what you find out and let the big boys clean up their own mess."

"What about the handler?"

He shrugged, "Don't touch him. If he's in on it, he'll get what's coming from his own people."

"I can take a sniff, see what stinks. But I ain't shaking down any made guys, there ain't no future in stupidity unless you're in politics."

Duke gives me an 'it is what it is' shrug.

"How do we know this guy on the inside?"

"We don't *know* know him. He's syndicate vouched by our backer, but I get the impression he's a name rather than a guy."

"Another outsider?"

Another shrug.

"What's the weather like elsewhere?"

"It's a dry spell."

"Fuck," I do some quick math, weighing the odds, squaring the angles, measuring the literage, "Call the backer and tell him I'll take a look for 15 and get back to him. Between you and me, though, I ain't swinging for the fence on this 1."

"I'll make the call."

Duke wanders outta earshot. Punches in a number on 1 of his burner cells and begins an animated conversation putting forward my counteroffer. The negotiation is far shorter than I thought it might be. I half-hoped the backer would back out at the ask.

Duke returns, leans against his Mazda, and smiles, "We're on. Easiest 15Gs you ever made."

I wasn't so sure.

# 6.

With a new burner, a tried and tested ID that covers any cursory background checks regarding my validity as an out-of-state thug, and Duke's St. Louis name's address and description locked in my memory, I'm as prepped as I'm gonna be—this is a think on your feet kinda deal, so the plan is sketch...

The name I need to make contact with is Bismarck Laidler—a name like that had to be a cover alias, right? Laidler's got a walkup apartment rented in Central West End, not far from the Cathedral Basilica of St. Louis and Forest Park. As far as Google's concerned, the local area is a lively place of bars, restaurants, hotels, clubs, boutiques, markets, museums, art galleries, and just a crow's throw away from Midtown and *The Furlough Casino & Lounge* in Kosciusko on the Mississippi.

I'm wearing a black tee and jeans, driving in my tan, soft-soled, Cole Haan Oxfords, laces tight in case I gotta run. I check the time on my newly taxed Rolex—3pm—it's my only bling, but I ain't convinced it's me.

I take a drive 'round Forest Park Southeast and Kings Oak and Midtown and Grand Center to get my bearings, cruising by a likely eatery—*Pappy's Smokehouse*—and a likely bar and club rich area—*The Grove.* I pin that information in my mind map for when I get hungry or thirsty, as both places are within walking distance of Laidler's apartment.

The apartment itself is sandwiched between the 1st and 3rd floors of a red brick-fronted building. The ground floor is a vape shop—*Venom Vapes*—with a cartoonish logo of a golden cobra spitting orangy-yellow vaper venom that spells out the vendor's sign above the door. I pull down a side alley and leave the Kia parked in a residential lot behind the apartment building, walk 'round to the front entrance with my leather grip in hand—my luggage grip, full of clothes, wash kit, and some personal shit like cell phone chargers and Bluetooth EarPods, I leave in the trunk alongside a paramedic 1st-aid kit (another just in case item) until I'm comfortable with moving in. From a watchful drive-by and a quick scan of my surroundings, the neighborhood appears blended with a white majority, so I oughta blend in with the locals without being a novelty. Next to the vape shop entrance is a door with 3 intercom bells—Laidler rents number 2.

I press the buzzer. I'd been told that my contact/roommate oughta be in between 3:30pm and 6pm.

"Yeah?"

"It's Logan," I present myself incognito—Logan Anthony is my AKA for the foreseeable.

The door buzzes and the automatic latch opens. I push through and take a flight of stairs to a 2nd-floor landing lit by a yellow courtesy light giving the stairwell a jaundiced ambiance. I drop my grip and wrap knuckles against the apartment door, wait while Laidler spies me through a fisheye peephole. Satisfied that I meet the description he'd be given of me, he opens the door—it's not a welcome, it's acceptance.

Laidler's in the life, but he ain't in my life and I ain't in his, so we're wary of each other. My host's 30, give or take, black-skinned, wide nose, mistrusting eyes, 5' 6", offset by broad shoulders and powerhouse legs, his head sports a short crop with a tramline clipped parting that nicks his right eyebrow. He looks like a lifter and swaggers like someone who can squat 300 but can't run 20 without his body sucking oxygen through every orifice. He eyes my 6' 2" gorilla frame and the obvious fighting experience etched into my features and nods—my eyebrow nick is scar tissue.

"You can come in."

I toe my grip over the threshold and leave it just inside a short central hallway, it clanks with tools. The flesh of my lower back is taking an impression of the Kimber Micro 9 while my new acquaintance and me feel each other out.

I step inside and close the door, "Mind if I take a tour? To get my bearings," I ask, I wanna know the layout of the place and check the closets and under the beds for monsters.

"Be my guest," Laidler invites; "Your room's 1st on the left."

I get the feeling he'd ask the same if this was my place.

"Right."

Laidler saunters into the living room while I heft my grip into my given room and hump it onto the bed. The bedroom's nothing fancy, sufficient for a double bed and a dresser—no closet. Back in the hallway, I crack the other bedroom door across the way: double bed, dresser, closet, PS5 wired into a 40" flatscreen, lived-in messy. Next to it is a white tile bathroom—no bath, just a shower and shitter and sink and mirrored wall cabinet (empty).

At the end of the short hall is a small kitchen with a counter dividing the open plan living space kitchenette from the living room where Laidler's lounging in a brown fabric easy-chair, sipping beer from the bottle. The counter has a set of keys on top.

"Cold 1 in the fridge if you want it? I eat out mostly, so I only got cereal and milk if you're hungry."

"Beer's good," I accept the hospitality, helping myself to a Coors. I find a bottle opener on the countertop next to the keys and lever off the cap with a hiss.

Taking a chair at a circular cream-colored Formica dinette table in what would be the dining area, if it wasn't all 1 with the lounge, I face Laidler in his easy-chair. There's a Bluetooth speaker on a similarly cream-colored coffee table in the lounge: no tunes play; the rest of the living space is bare of personality.

Straight down to business, "Who owns this place?"

"Guy who runs the vape store owns the building."

"You lease it in your name."

"In Laidler's name," he snorts derisively.

"Close to the casino," I'd reconnoitered Google Maps for the route before parking out back of the building.

"Not far, 10-minute drive."

"You work nights?"

"Mostly, gives me plenty of time to workout in the day. I got keys cut for you, they're on the counter, so you don't gotta rely on me."

"Fair," I'm jealous, I hadn't had a moment to workout in a week; "What's my in?"

"You're supposed to be a guy I know from back in the day looking for some heavy action. I put a word in, said I'd vouch. If he likes you, you'll probably pay rent running errands with me so the boss can feel you out."

"Such as?"

"Usual muscle stuff: dropoffs, payoffs, some driving around, periphery shit."

"How many on the inside crew?"

"12 guys. You got 2 at the top; 5 lean into the day-to-day; 2 bodyguard the casino boss and penthouse; another 2 get into the nasty stuff, and there's me. They're all Gs, but Mutt and Yo-Yo are real bad men."

"That's a lot of guys, even for a flash laundromat."

"I ain't counted the no-marks and hustlers on the street. All in, there's maybe a 100 guys getting paid."

"Sounds like empire building?" I frame a question.

"I think there's a move to carve out a piece of the St. Louis pie these guys don't wanna share with Chicago. The only reason Tricky's got keys to the vault is because he knows all the gaming angles to cheat and grift a casino outta money. As manager, he's 'sposed to keep the cheaters out and the odds in Chicago's favor. 'Course, if you know all the angles, you're gonna be tempted to make them work for you."

"Tricky?"

"'Tricky Ricky'—Riccardo Caduto. But he ain't alone in this, Chicago's made man is making moves alongside."

"A 100 on the payroll's a lot of action, maybe they've taken a bigger bite than they can chew?"

"Maybe... the pie's red-hot and it's gonna burn their lips if they ain't careful. They need to strengthen their position with the locals and out-a-town suppliers if they're gonna break away from Chicago."

"If the hitters are busy on the make who's running security in the casino?"

"They got a legit monkey jacket security firm covering the casino floor and exits. But Tricky don't trust just anyone 'round the counting room, vault and offices, he headhunted a few guys from the legit firm to form a tight unit behind the curtain. He's pretty paranoid about Chicago, could be all the coke he's been pushing up his nose, could be he's a savage when it comes to money. I only got in because I'm backed. He knows me through Chicago, but he doesn't know you: the word went out for the 411, a name said they know you from Metro East, but it's smoke. I vouched for you, but he ain't trusting you anytime soon, might even think you're a plant or something. He'll bring you in to see what's what, but he'll probably push you out just as quick."

I wouldn't say driving to St. Louis is a wasted journey, I'm banking 15Gs for my effort whether I get inside for a peek at the St. Louis operation or get shut out, but I do wonder if it's worth unpacking?

"What's Tricky like."

"If wishes were bullets, he'd be shot to death. But guys like us are loyal to the money and everyone's making bank, so he gets a pass. He lives at the casino. He's got a suite on the penthouse floor on the 3rd, him and his boyfriend. The top floor operates as a private hotel for high-rollers and where the Chicago bagman stays when he collects the laundry. 1st-floor is admin level and a few champagne rooms for the house hoes to rinse your balls after the tables have rinsed your wallet. There's underground reserved parking and utility level below the gaming floor. The rest of the place is legit; apart from a weekly no-limit card game held in the penthouse lounge that the commissioning board ain't in on. The floor manager's Chicago's fixer, he sidelines as the casino pimp and deals a small amount of drift to the rollers and a lot of snow on the streets. His name's Dave Fortuna, but he's known as C-Note."

I cocked my head why?

"Fortuna 100—C-Note," Laidler enlightens; "He's the other guy angling for power, but he's a cagey motherfucker. Some of the gambling machines have been rigged; some for taking a higher percentage than permitted and some for washing dirty money and paying out clean. The champagne's knock-off stuff. Yeah, there's plenty of side hustles. The bank's regular, but there's a leak pissing profits like a sieve hit by a sawed-off."

"How much?"

"About 30 to 40 a week, double in hustle. It ain't lazy income, there's a lot of outgoing, but the interest's rolling in."

"Fuck, that's a straight-out mugging. Are you sure Tricky's shorting the take, or is there grift he's not in on? Maybe it's all C-Note or an inside man you ain't figured... the bagman passing the blame back down the pipe?"

"That, I don't know. I've been connected to the operation for 3 months now, and I still ain't trusted in the vault or penthouse."

"3 months?"

"Yeah, and it's been a bigger ball ache than rehab. Lifting weights and drinking a few beers is my only release, I ain't even got a freebee from 1 of the casino bitches C-Note's got on a tight leash."

"How long's Tricky been running the casino?"

"5 Years."

"C-Note, the same?"

"Yeah, they came to Louis on the same bus."

I did the math, and near as dammit come up with 10 million reasons why the big boys wanted some hard accounting done—10,000-liters, that was double the gas money Duke and me got told was leaking.

"It's payoff money."

"What?"

"From what you say, it looks like Tricky and C-Note are here to stay, so it stands that they're investing in the local market. Drug buys ain't cheap: you got local law enforcement to grease, you got lawyers on call, you got legit business fronts, you got stash houses. Buying into St. Louis gotta be a million $s upwards money on the table deal, right?"

He says, "Right," but infers obviously.

"OK, a lot of Chicago's moneys on the street, so we don't gotta find the skim, we gotta find out where it gets spent?"

"Yeah, yeah. We could do that. We're on the outside and so's a lotta of the cash: we knock a few heads together and find out who Tricky and C-Note's in bed with?"

"Even taking into account the spread needed to buy into the game, these guys are working returns on their deals."

"They ain't fucking around."

"If you're shorting the organization, you better get organized or organize a funeral plan… this is a big move."

"I'm driving Mutt and Yo-Yo to a meet tonight; I think it's a money drop. I might be able to get some choice information."

"I can follow, then follow the money; see where it ends up?"

"That won't work, Mutt and Yo-Yo'll clock a tail a mile off. They're good at what they do, that's why I drive, and they spot."

"What then?"

"I'm meeting up and heading out from the casino. I'll introduce you tonight so you can feel the place out for a few hours. We'll figure out a workable plan to follow a payoff next time."

"Next time?" I worry, I got maybe a week before I got found out or kicked outta the city.

"Man, there's dropoffs and pickups every night, we don't gotta wait long."

"Fair. We'll do it your way."

"How much you getting for this play, anyway?"

"Enough to take the risk."

Rack nodded, slowly. His lips turned down in a pensive DeNiro frown, "That much?"

Fuck... I oughta have asked for more.

# 7.

I get my luggage grip from the car. Take a shit, a shower, a shave, and then roll a pillow under my neck and grab a couple of Zs. The bedroom door got no lock, so I rummage for a chisel in my tool grip and wedge it underneath to slow down unwanted guests long enough for me to chamber a round into the Kimber and drill 9mm holes through the door panel, splintering anyone with bad intentions on the other side with wood chips and lead. When I wake, I splash on some cologne, deodorize my pits, and pull on the suit jacket Duke advised would give a good impression of an old-school bad guy who knows his way around a casino—I don't.

I know enough about gaming to throw chips onto the felt and ask for cards. Never quite got my head around craps, I know how to bet at roulette, and my math is quick enough for blackjack. A few years back, I provided security on a backroom 3-draw poker game, so I picked that up, but I'm no fucking sharp, and I fucking hate fucking losing.

Refreshed, but hungry, I take a walk over to *Pappy's Smokehouse* on Olive Street and feed myself a large pulled chicken and brisket sandwich on a soft bun with sweet potato fries, careful not to get any sauce on my get-up: white shirt, blue jacket, dark blue suit pants, cool brown Oxfords.

Getting a table between the lunch and evening rush ain't no more than a 5-minute wait. My work routine ain't routine. I don't got set meal or break times. I grab food whenever I'm hungry rather than at a certain o'clock. My appetite's adjusted to antisocial single-o eating, the jams of regular breakfast, lunch, and dinner ques are enough to give me indigestion. There's no unsavory jams at *Pappy's.* Service is almost as swift as I am at demolishing my order.

I ain't trained hard in a week, the everyday physical maintenance of a 100 knuckle pushups and a 100 abdominal crunches don't count as proper exercise. My body, however, still craves calories like a bear getting ready to hibernate. I walk over to the diner because Laidler's gonna pick me up on the way to the casino. Apparently, he won't be seen dead in a Kia, my ride no more to his taste than it is to Duke's. Jaywalking benefits my general sense of direction, gives a feel for the streets around the apartment just in case I gotta duck down an alley or hop a wall to dodge pursuit.

My host asks me to call him 'Rack'. A tag earned from racking the weights at the gym, he tells me. Another G with another nickname: every fool on the street wants a tough AKA for kudos. For all I know, Rack could've made up his own dub to wear like gansta Kevlar. I got given my dub, but my AKAs cool enough to sound G, so I let it hang.

Before I leave for lunch/dinner (Linner?), Rack and me work out the details of our fugazi connection. I'm a freelance muscle-for-hire name he knows from his disreputable past, a no-nickname name looking to get in on some bigger action than the nickel-and-dime collections I'd been doing for low-rent loan sharks around

Illinois. Chicago's St. Louis handler, C-Note, asks if I'd be useful when Rack mentioned me, a euphemism for clearing dirty work. He's told I'm a standup guy.

When my burner ringtone chimes, I check the caller ID—it's Rack—his number's in my temporary contacts list on my temporary cell phone.

I wipe sauce from my fingers on a napkin, "Yeah?"

"Outside in 2."

"Right."

I pay the bill and drop a tip. Pat myself down to make sure I got everything: wallet with bogus ID, cell phone, keys to the apartment, buckle knife. What's a buckle knife? Well, it's a small lock knife, about 2 inches unfolded, that tucks behind a belt buckle. I ain't carrying a heater, the Kimber's snuggled in with my underwear back at the apartment, so I carry the stumpy knife on me for you never know.

Rack pulls up in a lip-gloss red '18 BMW M3 with black rim low-profile alloys, which is ironic because the car is anything but low-profile. I hop into the leather upholstered rider's side and Rack revs into traffic, taking Olive Street down to North 4th Street, Lombard Street onto South 1st Street, winding round onto South Warf Street along the river with s's and i's and p's dropping out its ass. Hip-hop tunes reverberate through an OCD-clean interior. I recognize the beats but can't tell you the artist. Conversation is all business. We ain't buds. I'm a mercenary and he ain't taking orders from the hired help.

4 miles south of The Gateway Arch, *The Furlough Casino & Lounge* nestles into a spot between the more established *River City Casino & Hotel* and the *Horseshoe St. Louis* casino. They are the major players for the players on the west side of the river. *The Furlough* is a modest affair by comparison. Although it makes its own bank, its real purpose is as an organized crime ATM and laundromat. With that in mind, the customers' parking lot is almost maxed out. From what I can see of the entrance lobby through the plate-glass frontage as we drive by, there's a buzz about the place that implies capacity takings.

A neon announcing the casino to the city rests on a brightly lit marquee walkway that extends from a white stone, Greek-columned, edifice. A respectable fountain plumes a water fan that hides the valet parking station; where honored guests, high-rollers, and whales are collected by the concierge and given VIP treatment. We coast 'round to the southside, using a keycard swipe that opens an electronic gate to the employee parking and delivery area 'round back. From this side of the building, another neon at roof height shines brightly out across the Mississippi like a reflection in the water stating what fun can be had if you cross over to our side of the river. There's little industry out here at this time of evening. All the deliveries have been delivered; all the shift staff are concentrated inside. A few small groups huddle outside catching a breath of nicotine, but the gamblers are inside spending (losing) their money and the employees are inside raking up all that green.

"You're not heavy?"

"No, I'm light."

"OK. I'll show you 'round. There's a route through to the 1st-floor that avoids video surveillance. It's used by visitors from Chicago to get to the vault and back to the private elevator and down to the parking level without getting caught on camera."

"We can ghost it?"

"Only this 1 route. The private elevator and penthouse are probably blind too, but all other areas are monitored from a security video suite."

Another keycard reader swipes us into the rear of the building. Rack's BMW's carefully parked farthest from the employee entrance, away from any other vehicles with an empty space either side to protect the paintwork from fuckwit drivers who can't use their mirrors. I got no such worries about where I leave the Kia, I ain't emotionally attached to my mode of transport—ain't emotionally attached to many things outside my own skin. Rack keeps looking back at his beamer as we walk away, checking its alignment inside the white box crib he chose to leave his baby in. The automatic closer pulls the casino door onto its magnetic lock, blocking Rack's view across the parking lot.

A network of corridors and service elevators and supply rooms and kitchens and changing rooms and security offices and champagne rooms and double security counting room and cleaning services and cellars and heating/AC boiler room and emergency generator room and employee restrooms and breakrooms and admin offices creates a warren of industry that astounds me. To me, casinos are fun parks, places where you almost always exceed your limit and payout for the thrill of losing. I never appreciated how much goes into running a business like this before, even a medium-sized casino like *The Furlough.*

We take a service elevator from the ground floor to the admin floor on 1st, exiting into a neat corridor, painted cream, with doors running along either side. Rack points out the security camera suite, where an eye-in-the-sky surveillance team watches the patrons and employees, not only on the gaming floor but also through the service areas unless you're threading the blind run that navigates through the building.

There're no watchful cameras inside the vault either, where the Chicago bagman separates the cream from the milk, and the secluded penthouse floor is almost certainly another blind spot, where the high-roller rooms and Tricky's private homo suite provides exclusively self-contained accommodation—whether that accommodation is for an hour or a week or as a professional perk. The only access to that level of luxury is via the penthouse elevator, there's an emergency stairwell and fire door that opens with a master key or by pushing an alarmed bash bar on the inside, but only a handful of trustees hold keycards and master keys to *The Furlough's* wonderland. Dave Fortuna is 1 such trustee.

The flush panel door has a nameplate stating the occupant's name and titular position—*D. Fortuna -*

*Floor Manager.* How much C-Note has to do with the mundane admin associated with his assumed role is debatable seeing he's maneuvering, from what Rack told me, to annex local rackets and corner a fair piece of the St. Louis drug market. Somewhere along this corridor is the office of an underling doing the actual work assigned to the floor manager's office—probably for 1/2 the pay.

C-Note's door is locked, not that anyone will barge in on a syndicated gangster unannounced if they know what's good for them. Rack reverently knocks and we wait like naughty school kids outside the principal's office.

"Yeah?"

"It's Rack and the new guy I told you about."

"Just a minute..."

A minute turns into 5 as we kick our heels in the hallway. Rack doesn't knock again. If we're forgotten, we'll stay that way until C-Note leaves his private office on other business. After about 6 or 7 minutes, we hear a muffled cry from behind the door followed by a quiet minute or 2.

I look at Rack, he shakes his head—none of our concern.

The door finally cracks and this peroxide-blonde femoid, around 21 - 22, appears at the threshold enhanced by designer tits and an ass that rolls like grapefruits in a net bag. Her makeup is 1 smudge away from slutty, her zip-front black minidress an inch from indecent. You can just make out red knees through her stockings and her blue eyes blink with knowledge only an experienced pro accumulates. She squeezes by, probably to freshen up and gargle mouthwash before hitting the downstairs bar and lounge looking for hourly-rate boyfriend material.

In her place Dave Fortuna stands, looking me over as I do the same to him. Maybe 60, sparse hair—badly dyed an orange shade of brown—watery brown eyes you can tell need prescription to help see much beyond the 4 walls of his office—he's a vain son-of-a-bitch, too vain to wear glasses. His clothes look off-the-peg expensive, not that I got an eye for suits and ties and shirts and formal designer shit, but I'm willing to bet that a real connoisseur of tailored clothing would find high-class taste as lacking in Fortuna as they would in me. His tan shoes have tassels, can you believe? They jiggle like burlesque pasties when he walks.

"Come in," he beckons, his pinky ring catching the light—wise guys wear them like a club pin.

In the old days, a ring like this was sold to cover funeral expenses, apparently? Maybe today it's to cover gas money if a guy gets whacked and someone has to drive him out into the sticks and dig a hole?

Fortuna leaves the door and wanders over to an oversized oak desk, the chair still angled from the hummer everyone knows he's been given by the blonde but no 1's mentioning.

Rack shuts the door and we both stand in front of the desk, hands clasped in front of us, while Fortuna stuffs his desk drawer with a small, white powder-smeared mirror, a loosely rolled $100 bill, and a black VIP keycard—which had unquestionably been used to cut lines of cocaine—with *The Furlough* embossed in gold across its face.

"I'm told you're a guy we can trust," he opens, pinching any missed powder from his nose with a finger and thumb.

I shrug and do the downward smile DeNiro thing that says 'of course'.

"Rack vouches for you, but I don't know you."

"I try not to bring attention down on me."

He squints at Rack, then at me, there's danger in his stare, a man not to fuck with, "Don't we all?"

"Caution's my middle name."

A pause, "Alright, maybe we can use you. Nothing big to start, a kinda trail period, to see what's what."

"Fair."

"You're not here for any other reason I oughta know about?"

"Like what?"

We stare into each other's eyes for a beat, he don't expect an answer and I ain't about to give 1, but he wants to let me know that he's suspicious and I'm on notice.

"Take a wander round tonight. I'll tell the cage to spot you a 200 in chips as a welcome to St. Louis."

"Thanks."

"Hospitality's free, but don't take liberties. We'll talk again tomorrow about where you might fit in."

"OK."

"You can go, I got shit to do," he dismisses, picking up the desk phone and punching 4 digits for an internal line.

We leave the way we'd come. The elevator to the ground level is empty other than Rack and me. There's a drone of muzak ambiance being piped inside the elevator car. For some reason, though, the Funeral March is playing in my head like a morbid earworm.

"He knows somethings off," I say as soon as the doors touch and gravity changes inside the car when it drops.

"Yeah, it's a shitty plan."

"I'm gonna flush this shit down the pan, I ain't breathing in other people's stink."

"Look, wait out tonight. Have a drink and lose 200 at the tables. I'll find out what I can on tonight's drop and maybe we can figure an angle that doesn't leave skids in the pan. Remember, I blew my credit getting you in this far, I'm on the hook too."

"Don't leave me hanging, Rack."

"I'll be back before midnight."

"Mother fucker," I meant the situation as well as my inside guy.

# 8.

I give my alias at the cage and pick up $200 in 'Welcome to St Louis' chips. I take a breath of cool AC and scope the main floor. The place is bling. The overhead lighting bathing the floor in soft-focused dream state illumination designed to blur a gambler's perception of passing time. Patrons mill between gaming tables; groups congregate around hot streak winners; drinks are dispensed by pretty waitresses to lower inhibitions and thrift. Some customers are dressed for the highlife and some verging on being shown the door. Gaming machines whizz, flash, beep, and chuck out winnings with exaggerated clunking and clinking rhythms. Winners laugh, players concentrate, losers max out their credit cards. The place operates like a no-dance rule nightclub, where risk-takers and addicts are encouraged to indulge in spontaneity and character defects. Poker, blackjack, roulette, craps, wheel of fortune, all the ways to throw good money after bad are presented as an investment in good times and due reward.

There's a no-smoking policy on the gaming floor, but you can indulge at the bar and in the lounge but not in the restaurant. There ain't a no-drinking rule, anywhere, so I order myself a gratis negroni from a passing brunette because I like the idea of it. I tell her that I'm Mr. Fortuna's guest, and she's spurred into instant action. Returning with my drink on a tray just as I'd decide on a game to chance my gratis stake—3-draw poker, the only game I can stay in front to lose small.

I wander into the mix and take a vacant stool at a likely table. The dealer's a well-put-together 40-something, whose uniform blue vest strains at the front with a respectable pair of mama jama breasts and matching Latina hips putting tension into the seam of her pants. Her age is concealed with liberal makeup to attract the eye without looking like a clown. I dig her eye makeup, but she's missing that certain charm I look for in a mature woman—namely, wicked desperation and a lack of inhibition. However, the other gamesters at the table are enamored enough, or drunk enough, to divert more focus into flirting than on their cards, as such they're chips down paying her wages.

I'm down $100 for a spell, then up $100 from my stake money and feeling more reckless than usual by the time I've sunk 2 drinks. Even in my hot streak, our dealer, Marta, is keeping the casino's ante cool with loose chips from the losing hands. Winning is pure luck. Luck, and the fact that I'm betting sufficiently small that the house ain't playing against me when it can cash out 4 worse players. Every now and then the pit boss wanders over, confers with the boxman, who's keeping an eye on the winners and losers and swapping out dealers who're getting crushed. Our dealer's on top of her table, everyone's happy, especially me.

I follow the casino routine of bosses and security and waitresses as best I can, but no 1 stands out as wrong. I'm outta my element in so many ways that I feel like a loser even with a stack of winning chips in front of me. I got no 1 to lean on for information, no 1 I can sweeten with a paper president, I'm small-time here, like my bets. What I oughta do is cash in my winnings, reimburse Chicago the 15-liters gas money they fronted, and get back to what I do best—beating money outta people like sweets from a pinata.

Around 9pm I'm ready to take a break, maybe sit at the bar, have a smoke and consider my immediate future. A seat next to me becomes vacant and a slim, yet doughy, guy, around 40-5ish, with a black slick-back trying to cover a balding crown, and a manicured beard trying to hide a fat-boy-slim chin, takes the spot. He's tailored, his glasses are tinted mauve, his fingers click with diamonds and gold rings, his neck's choked by ugly gold chains and necklaces that look camp rather than street, probably because the guy wearing all this bling is indeed spotting brown. It's the casino boss, Tricky Dicky. I know him from the descriptions Duke gave me of the main Gs. Behind Tricky stands a bodyguard and a fag hanger-on, almost certainly his latest dick warmer.

"Mr. Caduto," I acknowledge.

This is no chance meeting. I figure the phone call Fortuna made after ushering Rack and me from his office was to this man, who's probably been watching me on the casino floor through a camera array situated around the vaulted ceiling—now the free play chips make sense, I'd been under surveillance as soon as Rack headed out on his job.

"I see you're on a winning streak, Mr. Anthony," Tricky glances at my stack, and I don't mean between my legs, and grins like a thick-lipped wrasse. His breath smells like he'd been eating ass and ain't done us all the courtesy of sucking a mint after tossing the salad.

He places a single $10 chip on the table and accepts a hand. I let the $20 I'd just won play. Our dealer looks worried for the 1st time. Should she play me to win or lose?

"Call me Logan."

"And how do you like our casino, Logan?"

"I like it $300 fine."

He laughs at that, it's not a pleasing sound, though his bum-boy simpers behind like a homo echo.

"Good, good. Any new friend of ours is a valued guest. I hear you're rooming with Rack; he's been an asset to the organization. Although, I suspect his loyalties lie with Chicago money rather than St. Louis wages, as I'm sure do yours."

"I'm from Metro East," I remain cool, even though it feels like both Rack and my cover have gone down the shitter—I smell skids.

"I spent some time in Metro, maybe we have friends in common."

"I never worked the casinos."

"My circle of friends is large."

"Max Crayford," I spin the only name I can think of from Ill City.

"Oh, Max. I know Max, we go way back. I'll give him your best next time we talk," he's good enough a player that I can't tell if he's bluffing.

"Yeah, do that," I counter-bluff, trying to appear unconcerned.

Whether Tricky's bluffing or not about his connection with Max is immaterial, I'm willing to bet that he knows someone who knows someone who knows Max. And that someone who knows someone who knows Max will ask Max if he knows Logan Anthony before the night's out.

I hold aces in my hand, but my mind ain't on the game. The player at the end folds and the bet antes up by 10 for those who hold for the call. I flip my cards. The dealer holds 3 kings and Tricky holds queens—my table stake is doubled, but so is the trouble I'm in.

"Good for you, Logan. I do hope your luck continues. Enjoy your... whatever it is you're doing here."

That settles it. Tricky's shown his hand and it trumps mine by a long way. He may have lost $10 at poker, but he's up 10-mil in skim and I ain't playing those odds.

I drop a $20 chip for Marta, she's easy on the eye and good at her job, and then I dump my winnings at the cash window and take a wad of notes. At the bar, I intend to smoke a cigarette and lean into my 3rd drink. I don't wanna wait around for Rack to get back from his drop, I want outta there. But he's my ride, so I wait, take the weight off my Oxfords on a barstool, and watch the room in the wall mirror behind the service counter. I'd just got my ordered drink when the reflection of a familiar peroxide-blonde femoid appears at my shoulder.

Setting her purse on the bar, "Buy a lady a drink?" she asks, her smile an insinuation.

"Sure," I agree, drawing the bartender's attention.

I'm tab free so I can afford to be generous.

She plonks her grapefruit butt on the next stool and orders rum and coke.

"I know you, don't I?" she slips into the patter of a pro easier than a greased pig passing through the bowlegs of a hayseed, with not a clue that she'd squeezed past me in the 1st-floor admin corridor an hour ago, fucking cokehead... wait, that might just work to my advantage.

"I'm Lexi, like the car," she leans in like we're sharing secrets.

"I think you mean Lexus."

"No... Lexi, not Lexus."

"Cool. I'm Logan, like the Wolverine."

"Cute, I like your eyes, they remind me of our family dog when I lived at home."

"Really? That don't sound much like a compliment."

"No, it is, I swear. Rufus was a huge rottweiler, really powerful; frightening if you didn't know him, cuddly if you did. He had these soft-brown eyes for his family and a hard scowl for strangers."

"Fair, I'll own that."

"Are you on your own tonight?"

"Just me and the bartender."

"Would you like some company? I can be your lucky rabbit's foot if you rub me the right way," she propositions, fiddling with her dress zipper so it buzzes down exposing her enhanced cleavage. Up close and nearly personal, she's had so much cosmetic surgery that she looks like a pneumatic sex doll who's taken a backhand to the lips—I feel pity rather than attraction for her.

"Tell you what," it's my turn to lean in, "I just made myself a couple of hun for a bump if you know where I can get some drift?"

"I feel you, baby... here," she unclips her purse.

"Not here," I put a gorilla mitt hand over her soft hand before she deals me a hit at the bar like a dealer throwing out playing cards across the felt.

"I'll meet you in the lady's restroom in a few," I check my watch, the showy Rolex, convincing her I'm a sap her ceramic dental money vampire implants can bite into and bleed.

"We could get a champagne room, no 1 will see what we get up to there, baby."

"And waste my lucky charm," from staying her hand I caress her forearm; "Let's get high and play the tables while I'm hot... 50/50 whatever I win."

That sells the idea. Lexi stands, pours her drink down her neck, adjusts the cling of her dress, grabs her purse, and sashays towards the lady's. I decide a smoke can wait 'til later.

I scroll casually through my cell for a minute. And then, like a man with a demanding bladder, I wander through a loose mob of punters crowding the bar. My roll in sync with some inner rhythm. I'm feeling gangster, looking for my opponent like I'm making my entrance to the ring. The crush of people either side of me is cut like a bow wave parting before a longship dragon prow. I guess I'm being watched without seeing eyes on me. I switchback into a discrete alcove separating the nearest restrooms from the main floor. The doors are ordered Disabled, Women, Men—no cameras in this area.

Once I'm hidden behind the partition wall, I jink into the lady's, reasoning that my tail would be a guy. There ain't nowhere else I can get to from here, so I'll be left alone to take a leak and picked up again after I'd shaken off the hose.

Lexi's waiting in the end stall. My luck holds, there's no 1 else in here with us. She drags me into the cubical and locks the door just as the entrance door swings and we're joined by a group of chatty women who go about the business of freshening makeup, emptying bladders like pissing horses, and discussing their chances of getting lucky at the bar rather than at the tables. Our private party is subdued by discretion. Lexi and me are pressed close enough together that it could be classed as foreplay.

I unzip her dress at the front until the lacy trim of a black bra shows. Under the strap I slipped 2 hun from my winnings, keeping the stake money for contingencies. Lexi's fake tit feels like a lie, but the smile on her fake lips is genuine. The deal is on, she pulls a Ziploc gram of white powder from her purse and offers it like a tidbit for a good dog.

I touch her ear with my lips, "Take a hit," I whisper.

Her dilated pupils sparkle at the gift. She opens the baggie and taps a pinch into the crook of skin between her left thumb and forefinger. The excited women have finished peeing and adjusting their faces and are heading out as Lexi takes a deep snort of pearl from the clam of her hand. She blinks her fake eyelashes slowly and smacks her lip filler smile, her eyes burn bright.

"Take another," I offer.

"Really?"

"Yeah, you wanna have a good time, don't you?"

"You're so sweet, a real gentleman."

"Hey, I just need to call my ride and let him know I found a friend so don't need picking up," it's a lie, I'm arranging the exact opposite.

"Sure," her lips purse in a cartoon kiss, and then she goes back to drifting snow into her bump niche.

"Back in a sec."

I'm outta there and heading for the stall farthest from hers while Lexi dusts the inside of her nostrils. Fast as I can, I pull up the cab service I'd already chosen at the bar and dial the dispatch desk, not wanting to use any service provided by the casino in case the driver's a plant.

"I need a cab outside the front of *The Furlough Casino & Lounge*... 5 minutes, that works... Logan... what's the driver's name... got it."

I hang up and scoot back to Lexi, who's surfing the tube of a cocaine wave. I gotta stop her from whooping and turning the cubical into a 2-person dance floor. She's so fucked up on blow that she'd blow me right there and then if I had time—I don't.

I take what's left of my gram, waste not want not, "I'm gonna take a quick piss and then we can play some dice," I bullshit.

"Let's go up to a champagne room," she entices, unzipping her dress and exposing her body to the navel, brushing her silicone tit with a false nail so the bills in her bra float free, landing behind the toilet bowl; "Fuck it!"

"I'll give you some space," I allow, exiting the cubical so Lexi can fumble around the floor for her money.

I hold the entrance door open for a group of startled women, who check the door sign in confusion, "Sorry, I'm in the wrong restroom," I apologize and walk away like a defensive end running onto a tackle.

Back on the casino floor, I take a long walk around the tables as though deciding where to drop my luck. I see Lexi sashay from the lady's to the bar like a cocaine-slim fashion model hiding party balloons up the front of her dress, she's looking for her John—I ain't there.

Judging ample time has passed between my call and the ETA the cab dispatcher gave for my ride to arrive, I take a swerve from the gaming areas, through the vaulted entrance vestibule, the ceiling suspending an enormous chandelier above me like a 4000-lumen meteor about to hit, through the glass main entrance door, under the marquee, past the fountain, into freedom. I spot my cab at the same time I spot my spotter making a call, obviously passing on info covering my escape and organizing a tail car.

"What's your name?" I ask the driver when he buzzes the window down.

"Terry. You my fare?"

"That's right, take me to *Pappy's Smokehouse.*"

"*Pappy's'll* be closed now."

I climb in the back, "I'm meeting someone there, it's kind of a landmark."

"OK."

The drive ain't far, just far enough that I think I make a tail but ain't sure. Traffic signals and street lighting has replaced daylight. I plan to avoid Rack's apartment, Tricky's guys already got that address. I'm gonna hop a few fences around Midtown and order another cab to take me to a club so I can swerve any heat coming my way. I'll pick up my shit in the morning and drive outta here as fast as my Kia can go without breaking the speed limit. Then I'll drop the car in long-term parking somewhere, drop my current ID in the trunk, and get a rental under Saint Greaves as soon as.

Greed—it was the idea of golden sand Thai beaches and brown-skinned Thai girls that turned me onto this job. I thought it was gonna be a small operation, exclusively run by a few guys to clean the dirt outta illicit gains. What it actually turned out to be is a colossal mistake on my part, and a war waiting to happen between Chicago and St. Louis. Fuck that shit.

I drop a 50 on the cab driver. I don't wait for change; I'm still 50 ahead and that's good enough for me. Out the door, onto Olive Street, I fast walk round to the rear of *Pappy's* where a car lot runs along the back between the *Center Ice Brewery* and a fenced-off grassy area I don't know. A chain link fence rises at the far end. I scrabble over like it's a marine assault course, landing in a crouch on the forecourt of a BP gas station on the other side.

Walk around the back of the kiosk, where my Oxfords hit North Compton Street sidewalk, going south turning onto Laclede Avenue, ending up under the Harris Stowe State University's Henry Givens Jr. Camus arch—I know this because there's a plaque on an arch boasting the fact. I need a landmark to call up another cab, I decide this is as good a place as any in a city I barely know.

It's too late for studious types to be milling around or zipping by on green e-scooters with bookbags, but campus security power between the university buildings on an electric golf cart. It's all very eco-friendly, and safe enough that I sit just outside the streetlight glare on a set of cement steps with yellow railings in front of a single-story glass-fronted university building. I order another cab from another service, which removes me 3X from any pursuer's ability to chase me down, and light a smoke, my last in the deck. What next? A club or bar where I can spend a good deal of the night hidden in a crowd seems like a good option, and, better still, somewhere I can down another drink.

I call up Duke while I wait. I gotta warn him about the setup and knockdown that's coming. He knows shit's serious when I make contact this soon.

"What's up, Halo?"

"Duke, I'm bailing. This whole job's a ringer."

"Serious?"

"Fucking A, I'm serious. This thing's 10-mil upwards heavy and none of that weight is being kicked up to Chicago, who ain't proof positive if it's Larry, Curly, or Moe taking the take. I think our backer sent me in to stir up a hornets' nest. When the stinging starts you and me are gonna be loose ends."

"What the fuck do we know?"

"Me, not much. But you, you know who's asking questions, or asking questions for someone at the top of the food chain, and I know you. Listen, if I'm right, St. Louis management is planning to split from Chicago, or at least a major part of the organization. Someone in the syndicate's spotted the crack and stuck a crowbar like me into it hoping to lever the break wide open. Anyway, whoever contacted you doesn't want St. Louis to know who's maneuvering against them. I don't know much, but you know more. So, if I get got by St. Louis and they make me talk..."

"...I'm next on the list."

"Yeah, and if I get away clean, the guy who set us up got you on his list and I'm on your list, and there's an easy way to cut that list short: you and me get discreted. You feel me?"

"I'm starting to, brother."

"You got a name on our current employer?"

"He calls himself Mr. Black, but it's a dub."

"What does the manipulative son of a bitch think this is *Reservoir Dogs* or something?"

"Or something. It's insulation. He's obviously keeping his profile low."

"Yeah, but you and me are likely to die from exposure out here. Text me his number, just in case. And then pack a bag and get outta town until we sus this out. I'm quitting St. Louis in the morning when the coast's clear to get my shit. I should've never unpacked. I'm gonna ditch the burner once I leave city limits and get rid of the car as soon as. You oughta do the same."

"Aww, not the Mazda, I just had it wrapped."

"You'll be wrapped in a shroud if you don't."

"I'll change the plates," is all he'd consider; "What about our contact down there? You think he's in on it?"

"Nah, I think he's as expendable to Chicago as you and me. If I'm burned, he's gonna feel the heat from this dumpster fire before too long, maybe even tonight. 15Gs to take a look? Should've known you don't get money for nothing."

"You're right, and the backer gave up another 5 easy when you pushed the original 10. This shit's been rolled in glitter so we wouldn't notice the stink. Alright, use the emergency email to get in touch when you're situated."

"Gotta go, my ride's here. Keep your back to the wall, brother."

"Safe, Halo."

We both hang up. It'll be the last time we speak on these phones. Duke's probably fucking up his cell as I grind out my cigarette and walk to my cab.

"Saint?" the driver asks.

Logan Anthony is a bad memory I chose to forget. I bury that name along with any ideas I got about making an easy buck.

"Yeah, what's your name?" I question to confirm it's the driver dispatched for me.

"Gary."

I duck into the backseat of Gary's cab, "I'm your fare. Drop me off at The Grove?" I decide I'll cruise the nightlife around the area I drove through when I arrived this morning, feeling it's sufficiently far, but not too far, from Rack's place.

"The Grove, that's like 2 minutes away," he complains.

"It's a $20 tip away," I incentivize.

"OK, enjoy the drive," he irons.

I settle into the backseat. I ain't in a walking mood. I'm in a drinking and fuck you mood.

# 9.

My cab drives under THE GROVE illumination, a large yellow burst neon signpost with white lettering overhanging the roadway, marking entry into the Manchester Strip business district. I don't know this when I ask to be dropped off here, but the Manchester Strip area is the place to hang if you're into tasting the rainbow or art or cycling or all 3. I didn't cycle in. I ain't window shopping for art. And I ain't into sucking Skittles.

Like a herd on the move, humanity in numbers is a confusing blur of all stripes and colors. Judging by the colors and stripes of the Manchester Strip herd, a conservative suit jacket'll stand out like a pimp at mass, and I wanted to disappear. I don't know anyone, so I resign myself to hoboing the bars until kicking out time, and then roughing it on a park bench or something until daylight gives me a clear view of my surroundings and those who might be surrounding me. When the herd wakes up tomorrow and is on the move again, I'll blend in with the morning traffic, get my shit, if it ain't already got, and get out.

After paying the fare and tipping 20, I dump my jacket under an alley dumpster—so I can get later—roll up my shirt sleeves—casual—and wander the strip looking for a suitable place a hetero man can wander off the street into and not stand out like a straight prick at a gay wedding.

From the sidewalk, the *Chromatic* seems to fit my purpose. Large enough to absorb 1 straight guy into the crowd, and busy enough with a spectrum of homos, drag queens, trannies, and whatever to leave me to myself while they chase each other's tails. There's little to no chance of running into a fat-ass Debbie type or a mama jama croupier and charming my way into her knickers and possibly her place for a sleepover, straight women on the prowl for straight men are as rare a commodity on the Manchester Strip as finding an un-self-intitled millennial. Fuck it, the venue's as good a place as any to hide out, and I ain't here to party.

The place itself is extensive, with a large barroom, 2 expansive patios, an outdoor bar and stage area for karaoke, drag shows, and special events. Goodtime buzz and upbeat music amp the ambiance inside. I can't tell from where I stand at the inside bar if the outside stage is hosting karaoke or some lip-sync drag act miming along to a power ballad, which is a blessing to my ears on both counts. Not what I need right now: old bald queens with penciled-on eyebrows acting up, dressing up, and clowning up in drag with their big man heads flicking outrageously cartoonish wigs and their huge, shaven feet squeezed into Tina Turner pumps.

Even the bartenders are in costume. Skittles hair colors, loud tee-shirts, the guy who serves me is wearing a sleeveless, figure-hugging gold minidress that shows off a tribal inked left shoulder and enough thigh to catch a cold in July. He's applied ample makeup to feminize his already delicate features, and false eyelashes that could feather dust window blinds if he peeked through them. His dark hair is short and kinda quiffed, and his ears are pierced by a pair of gold loops; his eyes are blue in tonal contrast with his complexion, and his cheekbones have some kinda sparkly blush on them. If I don't know better, this one would pass as a mid-20s real woman, but I do know better so my flirt response takes a cigarette break. I give a 'what's up' head bob when he waits on me. He reciprocates with a genuine smile that illuminates the space between us with a stunning crescent of perfect white teeth behind ruby-red lips—I wondered if his teeth are also false?

"What'll you have?" he calls over the bustle, his voice feminine without being a parody or simpering.

I check the cocktail menu, it's pineapple this, grapefruit that, and lime the other—no thanks.

"Nothing with breakfast fruit in it. What beers d'you got?"

"Budweiser?"

"Anything but."

"We have Forest Park Pilsner, it's a local brew."

"I'll try that."

"OK, honey, coming right up," he touts for a tip with his best bartender service smile, bustling to fulfill my order.

On reflex, I can't help taking a quick peek at the tight little butt rounding the back of my server's figure-hugging dress. He catches me checking him out. I go red in the face... fuck, is it hot in here?

"Here you go... are you new around here?"

"Erm, yeah. 1st night in St. Louis. How'd you guess?"

"We don't get many straight guys in the bar on a Friday night."

"That obvious?"

"With some people, you get what you see."

"Not always."

"I'm a pretty good judge of character; better than you, anyway."

"How'd you figure that?"

"Well, I clocked you as a straight guy as soon as you rocked up to the bar, and you've been checking me out for 2 minutes and you can't tell if I'm trans or cis or none of the above, so you don't know whether to like what you see or not."

I'm confused. Is he saying that he's a she or is she saying that she's a he who identifies as a she or something else? Whether he's a she or she's a he they were outta my league, so I hold up my hands in surrender.

"Don't give up too soon, I'm into tough guys."

"How d'you know I'm a tough guy?"

"Honey, with a face like yours, you've either won a lot of hard fights or lost a lot of hard fights, either way, you're a fighter."

"Fair. And I generally win."

"I don't doubt it," he/she flutters their lashes and gives me the twice over; "This 1's on the house, welcome to St. Louis," they gift, settling my beer on the bar.

"Thanks, it's the 1st time I feel welcome since I got here."

"You here on work?"

"Yeah, but it didn't go too well... maybe my face put the client off."

"Don't see why, you don't scare me... maybe a little."

Unless I'm interpreting bartender banter bass-ackward, I'm being hit on in a queer bar by an undefined girl or boy whose sexy AF or not depending on whether their gender's opposite to mine.

"Cheers!" I raise my glass and take a sip.

"You like?"

"Nice. I'll have another later. What time does this place close?"

"Are you trying to find out what time I get off?"

"Hey, Erik, are you going to flirt with the straight guy at the bar all night or serve the horde," a fat queer in a pink tee stretched over the body type of a beachball asks in a tone of voice that recommends Erik get his/her ass in gear.

Is Erik short for Erika?

At the bar, the crowd's heaving with expendable income for drinks and appreciation for the tips jar.

"Keep your panties on, Del," Erik wisecracks, then leaves to dispense alcohol to the thirsty masses. Not before answering my question—sort of.

"I get off at 2 if you want to find out what kind of girl I am?"

Am I being ripped? Is Erik a trap? Not sure. What I am sure of is that it's quarter to 11: 3 hours until closing. I'd better mingle rather than try to figure out whether my libido runs hot or cold for Erik. Gawping over the bar like a slack-jawed moron taking a 2nd-grade biology paper exposes me for the ignorant straight guy I am.

I wander out into the patio stage area and laugh at the bad karaoke and worse drag act lip-syncs—not that I can do any better, my voice is somewhere between Vin Diesel and a gravel crusher. The formal show is supposed to be satire: the costumes, the wigs, the makeup, the glitter, the shockingly bad comedy, the sass, the audience love it. It ain't my scene, although, I gotta check my presumptions when bumping into some good-looking women, 'cause from a 2nd glance they turn out to be crossdressers and crossgenders.

To be honest, I relax into the vibe, everyone's out for a good time with no hidden agendas. It ain't such a bad way to spend an evening in hiding. And let's be real, I'm a tough guy, 1 of the toughest in my line, but I'm running the fuck away from *The Furlough* and every fucker to do with it.

Having downed my beer, I belly up at the bar only to be ignored by every bartender until Erik's free—there are glances, I think he/she has claimed me as their own.

"Another beer?"

"Sure, and have 1 yourself," I offer, it's nice to be a preferred customer.

"If we're having a drink together it's bartender's choice," he/she flutters their lashes, and looks into my eyes in a way that dragnets my soul.

"OK, your choice."

Erik taps painted nails on their chin in thought; "I have something in mind that'll satisfy us both, but you'll have to deal with a little fruit."

"Do your worst," I dare.

Heavy on the hard, light on the soft. I watch my bartender slice discs of orange zest, adding them to 2 rocks glasses and muddling the orange to release the juice. They drop a sugar cube into each glass, squeeze more zest onto the cubes to dissolve them. They add a liberal dash of bourbon into the mix with 3 cubes of ice, stirring to chill and blend. Then they take a sultry sip from 1 glass and smack their lips at the taste, adding another spill of bourbon, another whizz with a glass stirrer, and finally a fancy curl of orange peel for garnish.

Bright-eyed and animated, "Enjoy," I'm served the glass with my bartender's red lipstick taste mark.

Crap... do I drink or not? If Erik's a woman and I hesitate, then whatever this is withers on the vine.

I give her a look. A soul-searching look like the 1 she'd just given me, and I'm 99% sure that she's a her.

"I like the glass design," I compliment the red smear, taking a sip from that side of the glass to prove my appreciation; "Did you just make me an old fashioned?" I ask, after smacking my lips.

Leaning across the bar, "I may not look it, but I'm an old-fashioned kinda gal," she insists, blowing me a kiss and winking 1 fan of lashes; "Cheers!" she raises her own glass and takes a sip.

"Cheers," I do the same with the 1 we share.

I drop 30 on the bar, "Keep it," I tip.

"Erik... customersss!!" a reminder ricochets down the bar like a verbal bullet.

"Duty calls," she rolls her eyes.

"Catch you later."

"It's a date."

I take my Old Fashioned for a walk out to the patio to 'enjoy' the entertainment—either the singing and jokes have gotten better or I'm getting drunker, because I laughed once and tapped my foot 3 or 4 times. I buy another beer to keep a light buzz humming, washing out the taste of cigarette carcinogens. Erik has sparkling water, 1 alcoholic drink's her limit, she's driving home. I hang at the bar and watch her sip her drink through a straw to preserve her lipstick—the image is seductive. Erik doesn't strike me as a functioning lush, an easy slip working behind a bar. She knows what she's about, giving just enough attention to each customer to make them feel special, remembering a preferred beverage here, and a compliment on style there, she works the tips jar like the frilly $ bill strap on a stripper's thong. From the entire herd, only my name is asked and remembered. Every other nameless belly-up customer clamoring for attention is unworthy of that honor.

"Saint? You look more like a sinner..." she jokes, and then on the next breath apologizes, "...sorry, you must get that all the time?"

"Doesn't mean it's not true."

"So, you're a bad man?"

"When I gotta be, it's not a hobby or anything."

She looks dubious. Laughs. Thinks about it for a second, then shrugs, "What's your last name?"

"Greaves."

"Saint Greaves... San Greaves... El Santo... sounds sinister in Spanish."

"It's Heiliger in German."

"I guess you lucked out then?"

"I guess so... Erik's short for...?"
"Erika. It means eternal ruler in old Norse."
"Queen of the bar."
"No, that would be Del."
"I heard that, bitch," Del minces by; "Get back to work or I'll get you collecting glasses," he threatens.
"Better get back to it... do you want to, maybe hang out after closing?"
"With you or Del?"
"Me."
"Yes."
"I think you're cute, so I'd like to get to know you better. Just so you know, I don't sleep with guys I've just met."
"Fair. I'm only interested in your ability to mix cocktails anyway."
"Really?"
"Hey, I'm an old-fashioned kinda guy."
"Erik!" an insistent voice from the busy end of the bar calls.
"I know, I know! No rest for the wicked. Stick around after lights-up so I can check you out in the full-glare of unsympathetic lighting," she twirls on her feet like a dancer and waltzes along the service side of the bar as if on stage.
It's a better performance than the cat stranglers on the official stage, but I ain't gonna get an encore until the bar calls time and last orders are served—Del the manager is keeping tabs on the duration of our exchanges.
With the promise of getting to know Erika better, I stick around until the end of the night and the

round-up of lights-up stragglers have been rounded up and the rounding-up of calculated tips have been handed round, and the ambient glow switches to unsympathetic lighting that starches the interior space in bright reality.

Even after a busy shift, Erika's skippy and upbeat in her white Nike sneakers with a gold swoosh—she looks just as good in the lights-up brilliance as she did under subdued. I noticed how short her dress is when she was behind the bar, how could I not? But up close and personal, I can appreciate what a great pair of legs she has: smooth, tan, shapely, with muscle from deep machine hack squats, leg curls, and hip thrusts. They ain't ripped like a man's legs, that, and the fact she don't have capped shoulders and sasquatch feet, support Erika's provenance as a true-born female woman. The top of her dress ain't stuffed with c-cup silicone, there's a real pair of tits in there. Feminine features and behaviors really turn me on, but I really ain't into the whole tuck thing: I like my steak without sauce, my drinks without fruit, and my women without balls—fair?

Perhaps I shouldn't have got distracted by sexy cute, but sexy cute, single, and under 35 don't come on to me in my every day, and I ain't on the clock no more, so the hound is loosed.

I get a look up and down, "How tall are you?"

"6 – 2. What are you, 5 - 6/7?"

"5 – 10… in heels."

"I bet those legs look great in pumps. You work out?"

She takes the compliment with a smile, "You noticed."

"Couldn't help but."

"Thanks, I get to the gym 3 or 4 days a week. What about you?"

"When I get the chance... work gets in the way a lot."

"So, you're in St. Louis with work. What do you do?"

This was definitely a get-to-know-me interview; time to pull out the fake resumé, "It's a sad story."

"Will it make my mascara run?" she jokes, but she's unsure whether I'm serious or not.

"It might."

I got a cover story for contingencies, a story that covers where I'd fit into a law-abiding world if I was a law-abiding citizen, a cover story that still has some snap in the punch—my ego can't stand the idea of taking a mundane dive.

"OK, I'm listening."

"I boxed, pretty good, could've made money at it if I wasn't involved in a car crash... not my fault... but it messed me up for a bit," I ran a figure across my eyebrow scar to emphasize the semi-truth of my bullshit; "My doctor advised a year off for the brain swelling and injuries to heal before I stepped back into the ring. Then my old man developed a form of nonhereditary dementia: which made me rethink how much brain damage I wanted to voluntarily expose myself to," without confessing to a legacy of the work-related injuries, my cover explained the fighter's face I wore and the obvious physical wear and tear marked on my body whenever I got down and dirty with someone curious about my suture scars and cracked knuckles, "I kinda fell into selling sports equipment after that. Not so exciting, I know, but it suits my background, and I get free training in the gyms I supply," yeah, that's it, I speak fluent vague when it comes to giving out these kinda details. And, as I'm never in 1 place with 1 person for long, the depth of knowing me any deeper than 'what you see is what you get' is all surface.

"That is a sad story, do you need a hug?"

"Sure."

I got 1. A genuine hug I hadn't expected, thinking with my dick instead of my... I don't wanna say heart or emotional core or anything as sappy as that... but it feels good.

"So, I'm hugging a salesman?" Erika still ain't let me go; I get the idea that she's appreciating the hardness of my body.

"It's who I am inside that counts," I flip.

"Saint Salesman, the patron saint of Lycra."

"Through and through, like a candy cane stripe."

She steps back, "I'm sold, any free samples... I like jumpsuits."

I gotta think fast, the only thing I got in my car was a spare tire filled with fake IDs, cell phones, and cash, and a revolver under the seat, "If only I could hug out all my commissions, I'd be a rich man," I changed tack on the same wind.

"I'm not sure that'll go well in a sales meeting, you look like you could crush the air out of someone. You've got a dangerous vibe about you, Saint. A fighter's aura or something. It's the 1st thing I noticed when you came in. I thought, here's a guy the bouncers aren't going to bounce out of here if there's trouble."

"What can I say? I'm a killer salesman," I laugh.

"Killer at anything else?"

"Making-out."

"We'll see," she challenges.

"Hey, what's your last name?" I ask, she already knows more about me than 90% of everyone I've ever met, it's only right that I know a couple percent more about her.

"Wise," she fills me in.

Erik Wise sounded like 1 1/2 of a comedy double act, I guess that made me the straight man.

Erika doesn't leave her colleagues in the lurch; she tidies this and clears that while I down another freebie beer.

I'm getting knowing smiles and nods from the other staff whenever I'm in the way until Del gives Erika his blessing to shove off. She takes a quick restroom break, a reapplication of lip-gloss I note, and then I help her shrug into a faux leather jacket where I get a hit of perfume, something wild and way expensive.

"Night, babes," she calls across the barroom, partly so that everyone still working gets to see that she's leaving with a guy—not that I think I'm hot shit and Erika wants to show me off, although, I am kinda adorable if you're into slightly dogeared pugs—but to let everyone know we're leaving together. So, if I'm a psycho sex fiend, I might reconsider chopping her up into bite-sized pieces because a bunch of queens and queers have waved us off. Not being funny, if I wanted, I could roll the joint for every penny, as well as their tips jar, and this lot couldn't do a thing about it, and I include the hired security muscle in that scathing estimation.

"Don't do anything I wouldn't do!" Del calls out, toodelooing a farewell at his departing coworker.

"That doesn't leave much to the imagination," Erika discloses, bumping shoulders with me in a conspiratorial way.

Gentleman that I am, I walk her to her car, having the privilege of exiting through the rear patio area and not out the front entrance with the chumps.

"Downtown St. Louis can get crazy at night. The Grove's pretty safe, but Midtown can be trouble, so I never drink so much I can't drive home, just in case something spills east," Erika tells me as I follow her to a shared parking area reserved for *Chromatic's* employees and a couple of neighboring premises.

(1) I follow because I got no Scooby where we're going. And (2) I'm captivated watching her miniskirted ass roll beneath the hem of her jacket.

"Seems like there's trouble everywhere you go nowadays. I getting outta the States for a break from it all," I let slip, not admitting I'm definitively part of the problem and absolutely not part of the solution.

"You have anywhere in mind?" she asks, fishing in her jacket pocket for a bunch of keys with an orange ball fob on the end.

"Somewhere chill. Walking distance from a beach where you can sink a beer and listen to the waves roll in," I volunteer; "I'll decide where when I get a bit of cash behind me. I'm not set on anywhere particular, so long as it's got a warm ocean, great food, and bartenders who can mix Old Fashions, then I'll be swimming in gravy as well as salt water," I don't mention Thailand, as that might call into question the idea of finding a Thai girl 'wifey' and paying them 'housekeeping' to take care of my needs.

"Sounds amazing. I could use a vacation like that myself," she agrees, turning to face me and leaning her little butt against a Red Kia Sportage; "This is me," she smiles, an invitation to impress sparkling in her eyes.

"Nice car," I admire.

"You like it?"

"Not as much as I like you."

She's about to reply, but I cut her off with a kiss, leaning my body into hers. Erika's mouth responds instantly. It's soft and warm and generously adept at kissing that we sync as soon as our lips touch. I search for her tongue with mine. Just a flick, I ain't testing her gag reflex. I get an erection right away, it presses into her, she presses back. Fuck she's hot. Her hands explore my arms and back, settling behind my head to pull me deeper into the kiss. I, a typical man, grab her booty and pull her body into mine. If we were free divers, I think we'd have broken a world record because we don't come up for air for... well, longer than I'd kissed anyone at 1 time leaning against a Kia before. We carry on kinda dry humping like amorous teens without a curfew, until...

"Oh my God, get a room you 2!"

It's Del and the security staff. Having banked the cash in the night safe, given the bar and patio a walk-through—a morning cleaning crew will deal with the debris left by the partying horde—locked up and armed the security system, they'd finally ended their shift and were heading home for cocoa and bed. Some of them give an enthusiastic cheer like we'd scored a little league touchdown, and then car doors are slamming, and engines starting, and vehicles leaving.

"What about it?"

"What about what?" I'm in a lustful daze, Erika's eyes lock onto mine with the heavy pull of sexual gravity.

"D'you wanna get a room... back at mine?"

"Can you give me a minute to think about it?" I joke.

She takes a breath of fake shock, her mouth wide, her lips redder from kissing than from lip-gloss—I guess mine match hers, having rubbed lips for the last 5 minutes.

"I think part of you has already made up his mind," she assumes, not wrongly, glancing down at the crotch bulge pressing into her and gauging that my hard-on's at peak attention.

Yeah, I can't bluff this tell, "I don't need a minute, I'm in."

# 10.

Erika's done driving for the night so she can take a hard 1, pouring 2 whiskeys over a chill ice rockslide. I take a moment checking her place out. It's so small that the tour don't take more than 30 seconds. I invest time having a gentleman's wash in the cluttered bathroom—cleanliness is next to sex godliness. Erika drops a Bluetooth beat into a sound system from her cell phone, vibing *Down on me* by Jeremih, raising the tempo of the 1-bed apartment while she dedicates 5 minutes in the bathroom once I'd done, touching up her appearance and lady ablutions, I guess. She's meticulous with her makeup, but I can see through the foundation that she's not a pig-to-princess-to-pig trap, there's natural beauty under the mask of product. I like overt glam, but I like to wake up next to a good-looking naked face too. Yeah, I'm a hypocrite, my face don't get better whatever time of day or night, but I don't fuck myself—no matter how many times I've been told to.

1/2 a tumbler of whiskey is enough for the taste of alcohol kissing to move into enthusiastic groping. I lean into Erika's personal space to clink a 'cheers' and she farther into mine for a hot kiss and then a sultry kiss, spilling whisky over my hand. My single malt hand is taken and directed to her mouth, where each finger, in turn, is pulled between her lips, sucking longest on my thumb in a way that's so erotic that I thirst to perform a similar act on a female appendage.

Shoes are hastily, hoppingly, removed. I cup her face, run my fingers through her hair, pulling back gently so I can dampen her throat with sultry breath. The intensity of her touch seeks the muscles of my chest and shoulders; mine seek modest breasts and hardening nipples. Desire has swollen into physical expression. Sensual impulses rush the dam with a 2nd wave of excitement until the pressure of want overspills into need, flooding our senses with reckless confidence. Hands explore below the waistline. Resistance turns its back on respectability. Erika wriggles outta her tight dress, and I wriggle her hips and ass and pubic mound outta black panties, dropping them to her ankles so she can kick them free. On my knees I scrape a rough palm over her smooth inner thigh, sending a thrill through her core. She gasps when I slide a hand over the muscle belly above the V crease where thighs meet hips, brushing my fingertips over responsive flesh.

In my mouth, Erika tastes saline, her vaginal peach is soft as ripe fruit. Her body comprises smooth contours and the enhanced tightness of a gym-bunny butt.

She stands astride with me kneeling at the altar of her womanhood. My mouth worships her like a goddess. Hands entwine my hair as I nuzzle into the ecstatic dell. She thrusts, I grasp her rounded buttocks. I don't give head to the usual randoms I turn inside out, but this is mutuality, unspoken quid pro quo. In the bedroom, reciprocation involves oral stimulation of every erogenous zone yet stops short of penetration. We are mirror opposites in position and response; not least in the reflected devotion given to the corresponding parts of arousal—tongue for a tongue, cock for a pussy, nipple for a nipple. There are no more layers of inhibition, every stitch of clothing is peeled to expose the pith of unwrapped desire. It's a desperate thing, this beast: savage in its focus, primal in its intent.

No lies are spoken by exploring tongues, no smiles of insincerity from teeth and lips running over the summits and into the hollows of writhing muscle and briny skin. The smooth weight of her feminine ass. The sweep of my masculine biceps. My pectorals, her breasts. Erika exhibits an anatomy of beauty that only a lover can truly appreciate. The heady musk of her sex. The taste of metallic salts and viscus satisfaction she candidly leaks from rampant pleasure. As an enduring tide, my tongue laps rhythmically, patiently, relentlessly, inundating her senses. My head buried between her quivering thighs until she's swept away by the current. No need for verbal direction, the course of Erika's destination is guided by the physical act, her mind is merely a passenger in the vessel of her body, and I am Poseidon controlling the waves. *Down on me* transitions through *Lollipop* by Lil Wayne through *Freek-a-leek* by Petey Pablo into *Booty on her* by Lexy Panterra.

Ultimate pleasure stimulates orgasmic release. Fluid in the form of abrupt, irrepressible pulses gush from Erika's erotic core. There are pleas to the holy trinity. The communication of unanticipated expletives, the clamp of her quivering thighs against the sides of my head, the pull of her fingers in my hair, the unique tang of her release is an experience for the senses of the mouth.

After she's recovered from the high eroticism of anatomical response, the tension in her thighs and fingers ease. She is kissing me, tasting herself on my tongue, inviting the rigid curve of my penis into the vale of her pubis. A condom from the bedside drawer rolls over my rigid desire. She is wet, her body is willing, her vagina wants to possess an insertion of manhood. Erotic permission is whispered into my ear. No thought given over to the depth of our relationship, the appeal of instant allure is both shallow and profound. It is a cardinal temptation, both animal and human in its consummation. Masculine gratification positions at the entrance of Erika's open yearning. There is no resistance, we are matched, we slot together as if designed by a higher being.

Fucking is not devoted to a single act. There are many positions available for the young and supple. We tumble from saintly missionary to sinful doggy, to the edge of the bed with down on me dirty grinding. I'm sat with my feet on the floor. Erika's giving me a penetrative lap dance. I run my hands over every inch of exposed flesh. I'm mesmerized by her twerking motion. The visual in tandem with the physical is too much to witness without repercussions. I rev into 5th gear, picking my lover up and spinning her onto the bed to finish what we've started.

My climax, encouraged by hot-breath cries, is not merely an emptying of overburdened secretions, it yields all-encompassing pleasure that surges up from the depths of my entire body—maybe deeper than that. Erika's hip thrusts complement my rhythm. After the indulgence of kissing, oral exchange, grinding positions, and energetic crescendo, my lust is discharged in a convulsive torrent. When I open my eyes, Erika's staring with exaggerated pupil dilation into my eyes—damn she has a way of really looking into a person. Her short hair is fucked messy, her makeup smeared, her hands are still clasping my butt as the tautness of my body eases. She sags, satisfied. She has been taken to a higher plane by the masculine potency of my lust. My wrapped erection is deep inside, it remains hard, jerking with post-convulsive ejections.

We are interlocked until our senses return from the hedonistic abyss of desire, and then we collapse side by side, our breathing labored.

"I, uh… that was some fucking make-out session, Saint," Erika gasps, wiping a lock of hair from her damp forehead.

"Yeah, well, wait 'til you know me better."

"Can you know anyone better than that?"

"Gimme 5 and another whiskey and I'll show you."

# 11.

Mopped clean and swathed in a fresh linin sheet, we lay twisted in each other's limbs. My semi-erection is a plaything Erika idly rouses until it stiffens. We kiss, soft, long, rousingly. She straddles my middle, taking me in hand, her mouth over mine consuming my groans with a hungry kiss. Her enthusiasm gains. Another condom is raided from the drawer. She rolls it over my erection with her mouth, bobbing her head a few times to push it down. She rises over me, angles my shaft until the tip lines up with her opening, and then sits with me fully inside. The sounds of inundated pleasure are as stimulating as the physical act itself. Erika begins to rodeo, soft, long, rousingly. The ride becomes intense, the tempo in time with *Another Nasty Song* by Latto. I clasp her hips firmly, matching the depth, trajectory, and speed of Erika's building intensity. Her palms push off my chest. When the rise and fall rocks and drops with gasping concentration, I know what's coming next—Erika is. She loses physical adeptness, sensations overriding metronomic control. It don't require much more stimulation for me to edge closer and closer to climax. I give 3 or 4 deep hip thrusts and I join Erika at the apex of sexual expression.

Our intention is to clean up—again. Erika has just finished a demanding shift behind the bar, and I'd just had the 2 days I'd had. Condom removed, I ball it in a Kleenex and send it with a hook shot into the waste basket.

"3 points," I celebrate, blink once, and don't open my eyes again until Erika wakes me sliding from a loose embrace.

She heads to the bathroom and takes a piss, the flush gurgling like a morning alarm to my own bladder. The bedside clock reads 10:08 across the 7-segment black LCD. I oughta get up, if for nothing else than to avoid pissing the bed.

I stretch across the mattress, digging the back of my head into the pillow until my arching back lets out a crick of relief just as Erika leans out from the bathroom, toothbrush in hand, rabid toothpaste around her lips.

"Morning, sleepy head," she smiles frothily.

"Hey."

"Do you want to grab breakfast?" she offers, though not as confidently as what she offered last night; "I mean, only if you want to. You might need to head off or something."

"Sure, I could eat. What d'you got in mind?"

"Pancakes. I know a great place."

"OK, I'm buying."

"I should offer a loan of my toothbrush as you've been so generous," she invites, whitening her bright smile with a few more brush strokes.

"Fair."

She tilts her head, "Fair?"

"Umm... fair's a sorta catch-all word for OK, thanks, that makes sense, a bargain, something cool. I use it too much... lazy, I guess."

"No, I like it. You should probably grab a quick shower if we're going to beat the lunch crowd. I'm skipping the gym today."

"Last night's cardio ought to count as a workout."

"Fair," she laughs.

"Room for 2 in your shower, is there?"

"Might be a squeeze," she winks, disappearing into the bathroom.

I hear the showerhead run and I'm under its jets in 90 seconds after jet-washing the toilet pan with liquid bling—I don't pee in the shower when I'm a guest.

Erika squeals when the water turns cold after I flush. I let the water pressure return and then my offer to soap all the necessary nooks and crevices and goosebumps is accepted as an apology.

## 12.

Clean, in a dirty sort of way, I sit opposite Erika in Shrewsbury's *Golden Oak Pancake House* smelling of the same bodywash, shampoo, and flowery deodorant as her. In the shower, there's enough body and facial scrub products to sand back the apartment's woodwork. Not that I'm complaining, Erika's skin has a regimen I could get behind—and did. I decline a squirt of the same perfume when we're drying, even though I'm assured that it's some ridiculously expensive brand.

After freshening up, I sit the bed pulling on day-old socks, watching my shower buddy diligently apply makeup, and tousle blow-dry her short hair at a dressing table crowded with a dozen shades of this and a half-dozen of that, lipstick for every occasion, false lashes, mascara, brushes, applicators, pencils, and things I don't even know what for. There's a shoulder-length brunette wig resting on a wig stand, its plastic head staring at me with blank eyes as I look on with fascinated eyes.

Erika slips into some sexy black lacy panties, no bra, and a pristine white tee I can make out the shape of her neat tits through. She wriggles her butt into a pair of denim shorts and spends a moment adjusting the fit with hip-sway jostling that jounces her breasts and booty cheeks.

Considering where we met, I ain't asked and she ain't told whether she swings both ways when it comes to sex: does it matter if she eats the bun or the hotdog or both depending on her mood? Not to my sausage it don't. Of course, if she had a sausage of her own that would've been an altogether different kinda BBQ I wouldn't wanna eat at. Mercifully, my buffet partner's all bun, no added mustard or mayo or ketchup disguising the taste of her edibles.

"You don't gotta do all that for me… you look fine fresh outta the shower as you do lathered in soap suds or makeup," I reassure, assuming all this effort is for my benefit.

Let's be honest, some of the women I screw need makeup to keep up their allure, but Erika ain't my usual catch. Athletic build, short hair, youthful looks, she's got natural glamor I lean into, a physical slant of curves and taut abs I dig. Her looks take absolutely no effort to appreciate.

"Really, this is kinda our 1st date?"

I laugh, but she's semi-serious. I get the impression, what with her working nights in a nightlife setting, that daytime dating's a novelty, so I change tack, "I'm into your makeup, but I'm just as into how you look without it."

"I kinda feel naked without it."

"I like you naked."

"Yeah, I got that, but I'm not going out without lip-gloss."

"If it prevents chapped lips go for it."

She paints her mouth in a pinky shade of gloss, "Do you want a touch to stop yours drying out?" she offers, holding out the lip-gloss tube like a threat.

"Nah, I'll share what you're wearing when you kiss me again."

"When *I* kiss *you*?" she questions the 1-way emphasis.

"Well, it did get a little uncomfortable how much you wanted me last night."

I fall back on the bed when Erika jumps off her dressing table stool, takes 2 running steps, and leaps on me, covering my face with pink kisses until it looks like I'd lost 20 consecutive games of kiss chase.

I've never claimed to be deeply romantic, or philosophical, or into any mythomaniacal bullshit advocating that someone with a great personality who hangs a face like a moose is the equal of someone gifted with a head-turning ass and a beautiful kisser.

Ugly is ugly no matter how much money a person has, how much influence they assert, how interesting their conversation, or, how funny their anecdotes are—I ain't never got a hard-on over a punchline. The same ain't true for beautiful people: they can be dirt poor, uninfluential, dull as dishwater, and without humor, and you'd still smash. For sure, guys will smash pretty much anything, even an old athletic sock, so ugly chicks do more than fair when it comes to getting some—10X better than ugly poor dull guys, anyway. That said, I like Erika through and through and not just on the surface—or from behind.

We finish getting ready, a lot quicker now the pressure to glam-up is off. Me? In everything I brought with. Erika? In another pair of sneakers from a pile of shoes heaped like a monument mound in the corner of her bedroom. I'd like to see the shape of her great legs emphasized by a pair of heels, but they're fire in denim shorts and any kinda footwear.

It's no more than a 5-minute drive to Mackenzie Pointe Plaza, a retail strip with the *Golden Oak Pancake House* situated next to a dental surgery for those sweet-toothed pancakers who can't say no to extra syrup and cream and sugar cavities. With Erika's Kia parked, we walk across a large lot up a set of steps, and into the restaurant between the pillars of a red brick entrance arch. As we near, I feel a hand wriggle under my elbow, we enter arm-in-arm. I sense a little apprehension at the gesture. It's a considered act, a measure of feelings gauged by a show of togetherness. But I'm cool with it. In an unexpected way, I kinda feel like a grown-up.

It's nice inside. Erika explains the restaurant has newly opened, so the décor's as pristine as the table seating. Understated arty stuff hangs on the wall with a couple of neon illuminations assisting the overhead lighting. True to her word, we slip in between the breakfast and lunch rush (that'll be brunch), bagging a coveted booth—thems the perks of unconventional work patterns.

We're seated quickly and choose to sit across from one another. Last night we'd been as intimate as 2 people can be, twice, and got very steamy in the shower this morning. Strangely, though, we sit like teenagers on a 1st date not quite knowing what to say, so we read the menus rather than force a topic of conversation that don't involve flirtatious banter.

"What're you having?" I wonder, an icebreaker, even though I'd already broken the seal on our relationship.

"Hmmm... strawberry and banana pancakes. You?"

"Country steak and eggs."

"No pancakes?" she's incredulous.

"I got a long drive ahead, so I need to fill the tank," I explain.

"Oh. I was hoping that maybe you might maybe stick around another day? I can show you some of the sites... do you like the zoo? I'll buy you an ice cream cone," the contrast between fully made-up night-time Erika and the fresh face with a touch of cursory lip-gloss Erika lends a certain optimistic innocence to the young woman sitting opposite me—even if straight innocence has been absolved between us, slanted tentativeness remains.

"Much as I'd like to, I gotta be somewhere else," anywhere else, although, under less complicated circumstances, I would've jumped at the offer.

"Where are you heading next?"

My answer's interrupted by our server, who takes our order with a smile and darts away to get it fried and flipped.

I divert the conversation, turning it back on Erika, who, I assume, doesn't have to make shit up to seem normal, "How long have you worked at the *Chromatic*?"

"Oh, about a year... I kinda fell into it."

"How so?"

"It's a sad story," she plagiarizes how I introduced my backstory and phantom employ.

"I can handle it if you can?"

"Del's a friend..."

"...Del the manager?"

"That's right, he gave me a job after I failed to make rent as a dancer..."

"...I knew you were a dancer when I saw you twirl behind the bar, you move musically, or something," I'm excited by my powers of observation.

"Unfortunately, not musically enough. I tried out for a few professional gigs, ended up dating a choreographer who promised the world, I just had to wait for the right opportunity and trust he would find me the right spot to showcase my talent... 8 months later, I find out he uses that line on a whole stable of mediocre dancers he wants to bed. Seems it doesn't take much of a compliment for me to trust that someone's genuine. I was so pissed, I confronted him at his dance studio where I dumped him and my dreams in a very loud breakup."

"Will you try again, do you think?"

"No... I love music and dance, but I don't quite..." she pinches her fingers together and squints 1 eye to show how close, or far, she was from making the cut, "...have what it takes to make a living at it."

"D'you need a hug?" it's my turn to imitate her line.

"That'd be nice."

We stand and meet in an embrace that has some depth to it. If I didn't have to scram, and there weren't so many brunch munchers seated in the *Golden Oak Pancake House*, I think I'd kiss Erika like I meant it. But I *am* going, and there *is* a crowd of brunchers giving us sweetheart looks, and our server *is* servicing our table with our order, so I just grin like a podium winner at the ego Olympics when we sit across from each other again.

The meal takes up conversation time, it's delicious and sustaining. Around mouthfuls, we talk here and there about inconsequential stuff: no politics, no news topics, no thorny questions about the future. We're just 2 people who'd hooked-up, had a great time, like each other's company, and were now eating breakfast after 10am but before 12pm.

I'm dabbing my mouth with a napkin when...

"Will you be back this way anytime soon...?"

"Not sure. Like I said, I'm trying to get enough money together for a long, long vacation."

"Do you want to swap numbers?" she looks into me, gauging my reaction.

I gotta think quick: I could give out the number of the burner I'm about to throw; that would end our relationship without having to end it—but that would be a coward's way out. I could say: 'I'm not coming back this way anytime soon', which is at least honest. I could've said those things.

Instead, I say, "Gimme your cell."

Erika fishes around in her bag, reels in her cell phone, then uses fingerprint recognition to open it like a novice. I take it and punch my number into her contacts, naming myself *St. Salesman.*

I give, “My personal number.”

Giving it says something about the level of attraction I feel for my 1-night stand, but I don’t know what it says about my intentions.

Erika’s eyes go girl just engaged bright as if I’d just proposed, which says something about how into me she is, or how into me she thinks she is, or something...? Her thumbs type out a message and send it to my personal cell, safely hidden in the trunk of my Kia, so I got her number also. She won’t tell me what she’s put in the message, but she lets out a dirty giggle that I bet it ain’t a Hallmark card sentiment.

I make good on my offer to pay for the breakfast-lunch combo and drop a tip. When we leave the pancake house, Erika holds my hand. A simple transition from taking my arm, but a complicating statement of connection. Complicating, because I’m supposed to be burning rubber and St. Louis bridges not frolicking through Mackenzie Pointe Plaza’s car lot with an overnight girlfriend bumping hips and smiling like she’s the cat who got the pancake syrup and the cream.

In her Kia, we kiss. I get hard. Her hand seeks out my erection. Before I know it, I’m getting a farewell hummer with people wandering to and from their cars none the wiser of our PDA (Public Decency Abandonment). Well, that scenario goes through my head, but Erika ain’t an exhibitionist slut, and I ain’t a compulsive sex fiend. I know when to focus and when to live loose, and I had to tighten my grip on loose living.

What actually happens is that Erika drives me to a 7-Eleven near Rack's apartment for 5 reasons. (1) I'm keeping Erika outta the bad air clouding my exit. (2) I wanna slow-walk 'round Rack's place to feel out the situation. (3) I'm gonna call Rack's cell phone from somewhere I can watch the apartment and stay hidden from view. (4) I really wanna buy some cigarettes. (5) I don't wanna leave my leather grip behind for sentimental reasons.

She pulls into the curb and idles while we say our laters.

I lean in and kiss her syrupy lips, "See you, 'round... you're my favorite St. Louis attraction."

"You know where I live, circle my place on your visitors map."

I laugh at that, "Gimme a minute to think about it," I reuse last night's joke.

"Now I know you're playing with me. Get out my car... but don't forget to call next time you're passing through," she reminds.

I get a hand on the door handle, "Hey, if 1 dream don't work out find yourself another 1," I encourage; "Don't let 1 sad story and 1 dick boyfriend stop you finding happiness. If you love dancing, find a way to make something of it. You just need a plan, is all."

"I'll think about it."

"Thinking's for academics who never leave school. You gotta get out there and take chances because 1 lucky break might change your life."

"Like I took a chance on you?" she jokes.

"You can do better," I motivate.

She smiles, knowing the truth of my appeal. Maybe she'd take my advice to heart, stop treading water and swim back to shore? It's better to fail with style than to succeed at mediocrity.

"I'm gone," I say, peeling myself away.

Without looking back, I hear the Kia pull into traffic. My entire focus is now on going forward.

With a deck of Mavericks in my pocket, I smoke 1 down to the butt while keeping an eye on the street and the vape shop apartment building where I'd left my grip. Yeah, I'm old-school when it comes to nicotine. Vaping? You can blow that shit out your ass.

Some parked cars, unoccupied. Some passing foot traffic, unaffiliated. Some questions, unanswered. Sometime later, I dial Rack's number, watching from a side alley. It rings for a long time considering the job we're working together, and that we ain't been in contact for nearly 15 hours.

"Yeah?" Rack answers, surly as ever, yet with an undertone of stress or pain I recognize from all the times I've been the cause of that undertone.

"It's Logan."

"I missed you at the casino, buddy. Guess you got bored waiting."

*Buddy*—what the fuck? "Yeah, found myself some entertainment that didn't break the bank," I stretch the truth.

I see the apartment window blind twitch, but nobody's twitching around for me outside, so I stay on the line.

"Good for you. You don't wanna overplay your hand."

That's as good a warning as someone under duress is gonna give.

"Sorry to do this to you, buddy, but I'm skipping town. I don't like the action here... you can keep my shit, I'm traveling light."

"I get you. Better luck next time."

"There won't be a next time, I'm a goner."

"Right behind you," he sympathizes.

I get the feeling that Rack's about to become a goner of a permanent kind. I hang up and send my burner phone to sleep. This whole deal's a splash back in the pan with no shitter paper. My balls were wet and my pants are down, but I can still shuffle the fuck outta here without leaving skid marks.

## 13.

Rack knows the life; understands there are risks involved at any level. The deeper you dig yourself into a criminal hole the more spoil piles up on either side that can cave in at any fucking moment. If it ain't a rival, the Feds, a snitch looking to make a deal or make bank, a civilian, or a vindictive ex, there's always some fuck in your own organization willing to kick dirt down on you and stand on top of the pile.

Rack had got caught between rival factions of the syndicate whose hole he'd jumped into and was about to choke on the dirt—hard. If our positions were reversed, then he'd leave me smothered in the heap of bad decisions that collapsed in on me and leave me buried under. And then he'd shore up the sides of his own hole to prevent it from becoming a grave. Plus, we don't really know each other. We hadn't bonded over our 1 and only beer together. He's not my people, our relationship is the job, not a partnership. So, his back is his lookout and mine is the sole responsibility of me, myself, and I.

The lock's old, the key a new copy. The noise in the stairwell sounds deafening to me as I turn the key counterclockwise to open the door. As slowly as glacier shift, I creak the door ajar by 1/2 inches waiting for it to be jerked from my hand by 1 of the apartment's less-than-friendly occupants. In my freehand I hold a stainless-steel Charter Arms .45 ACP caliber Pit Bull 5-round revolver—my only gun before I appropriated the Kimber, now a heavy piece I keep stashed in the Kia.

The TV's playing loudly. I know this is to drown out the sounds of a beating. It also conceals my approach until I'm facing a big, not gym big, but large white guy, 1 medium build, if you overlook the heavy paunch, white guy, and 1 short, but jacked, black guy zip-tied to a dining chair with a nosebleed from his wider than I remember nose pouring over his duct-taped mouth, and facial swelling from multiple digs that look like he'd had an allergic reaction to getting punched in the face.

"Your buddy's up and left you, Rack. Now you're the only guy we can squeeze the information we came for outta. What'll it be... hammer, pliers, saw, chisel, maybe an ice pick through the balls? This bag's got everything we need to make you talk," the shortest of the 2, the paunchy spaghetti eater, with thick black, steely grey hair that grows thicker down the back of his fat neck, and side whiskers that look as though wire wool has been stuck to his hangdog cheeks, lays out.

He points suggestively at a familiar leather grip bag found in the room Rack had given me, and now open on the circular dining table with 1/2 a dozen tools around it.

The other guy, a stockier, balder, version of his 'buddy' is leaning over his victim, wiping bloody knuckles on Rack's blood-stained shirt—the same shirt he'd worn under his jacket last night.

"Is that my grip?" I ask, the Pit Bull held on the 2 hitters.

Both men whirl, hands going for their own pieces.

"*Don't!* Pull heat and I'll put you in the morgue," the warning's no idle threat, they know it and they blink; "Drop to the floor, hands on heads," I snarl, experience having taught me never allow a killer to get their hands on a weapon. I'll take their guns from their belts myself.

Rather than crashing on their backs full of bullet holes, they belly up to the floor like unfit fatties at their 1st yoga class.

1st, I take the talker's gun, talkers are always the boss.

"Hey, Logan..." the talker talks the back of his head into receiving a smack from the Pit Bull's barrel.

I don't wanna hear negotiation or excuses, that time has passed, "Shut the fuck up, fatso, or you'll get a lead lobotomy through the back of your dumbass skull. I'm getting my shit and then you and dumbass number 2 are gonna sit quietly tied to a chair while I get gone, for real."

That calms the situation a bit. Belief that you're gonna live through a dangerous situation if you cooperate reassures the person you're having a situation with that once they take the humiliation you're dishing out they get to walk off a few bruises and live to tell the tale, or tell lies about what happened, or keep it to themselves—whatever.

Of course, I lie. My credentials as an enforcer are built on underworld respect and accumulated contacts. With Duke in the wind and me a marked man until this conflict between Chicago and St. Louis gets resolved, I got no way of earning unless

I go legit—fuck that 9-to-5 bullshit. The only way to stay in business is to act businesslike, and a hostile takeover attempt of my business premises, namely my physical self, by these sorry mutts, has to be countered.

With both their guns confiscated, I search for means to secure them, "Did you guys bring nothing with?" I notice they'd used my new roll of duct tape and my cable-ties; "I'm gonna have to tax you for the use of my equipment."

Even though he's in pain, struggling to breathe through a busted nose, and extremely pissed at the guys' face down on the floor, Rack sits still and waits to be released. He knows the procedure. I'd lock down the hitters 1st, then I'd come to his rescue. That's a professional gold star I glue to his gangster chart.

Rack levels up in my estimation from a name in St. Louis to our guy in St. Louis. I still might have to do him bad if his loyalty to Chicago complicates the situation, but I'll regret it more than I will for the 2 enforcers who were undoubtedly gonna tie me to a chair and beat what I know outta me before blowing everything I ever knew outta 1 ear... motherless cunts.

Rack's eyes, even the swollen 1, watch as I tie down his interrogators like they're roped rodeo calves, taping their mouths shut, and then rifling through their pockets for wallets, watches, cell phones, and weapons. They groan a lot. I stub my toe on their ribs for getting too vocal. I throw what I find on the dining table next to my grip. A few $100s in bills, a fob of keys, decent watches I can pawn for gas money, 2 flip-phones, an out-of-charge taser, 2 silenced semi-automatic 9s I drop the clips outta, clear the chambers, leaving the slides locked to the rear. I also discover a respectable brass knuckle duster, which might come in handy—pun intended. When I feel I got control, I turn my attention to Rack.

"This is gonna hurt," I warn, clamping his bent nose between the fingers of both hands.

Rack's eyes go wide, even the swollen 1, realizing I'm about to perform an amateur enthusiast's surgical procedure. He grits his teeth and bears the realigning intervention—he don't have much choice being tied to a chair—with resignation. Only after I'd righted that wrong, and Rack's finished mumble-cursing me through his adhesive gag, do I remove the duct tape covering his mouth. I ain't tentative. Like tearing off a band-aid, I just whip it free, tape adhesive waxing a few beard hairs in the process.

"Can I interest you in a new watch, sir?" I joke, holding up a couple of grands worth of black bezel TAG Heuer—not that this fucker would've paid legit for it.

"Fuck you and fucking untie me!"

"Fair. I think the bigger guy's watch'll fit me," I appraise. The watch has a lit red detailed wristband rather than a clunky gold bracelet. The Rolex ain't really my style. I wear it because I wanted to take it from Casey and it's worth something in resale. But it feels too flash on my thick wrist, like I'm trying to flex without a pump. Rack's not amused, "Do not kill these guys, I need a word with them," I caution, there's violence in his eyes, even the swollen 1.

"These pieces of shit need to pay. Motherfuckers tased me!" he spits, literally gobs from his chair onto his nearest assailant.

"When I'm done, I'll give you 5 minutes, but I'm gonna do a professional job on them 1st... you get me?"

"Yeah!"

"Yeah?"

"Yeah, I get you."

I loose the beast using my buckle knife and stand to 1 side. Rack remains composed and I nod—respect.

"Go tidy yourself up in the bathroom," I suggest.

"Man, my bruises got bruises, you got anything for the pain?"

He looks worked over, not so bad he can't wear the pain like a man—but some thresholds ain't as solid as a man thinks.

"Some coke," I flip as a joke.

He don't get my humor, "Let me have it," he holds out a hand.

I cock my head, stare into Rack's lumped-up face. I don't think it's a good idea, but something in his eyes tells me he'd been scared—deep. Death hadn't taken his soul, but the cold touch of the Reaper's skeletal hand on his shoulder has stolen his nerve.

"Just a bump to take the edge off," he whines.

What I don't need, is an edgy smalltime G for Gangster with a bigtime G for Grudge hovering on the edge of V for Violence right now, so...

"Here," I hand over what's left of the 8-ball baggy I'd scored at the casino, the zip has been riding my pants pocket for 12 hours; "Don't spend it all at once," I advise.

He takes it from my hand—a little too quickly. He'll have to blow the blood clot plug outta his nose before he can stuff the blow I give him up there. I hope just enough snow to give an artificial confidence boost. I doubt there's enough drift for him to disappear into the blizzard, but what the fuck do I know—thresholds, right?

"You and me need to clarify a few things," I warn the prone enforcers it's their turn to take some pain from a killer.

# 14.

Getting confirmation of what I think I know is easier than I thought it might be. The smallest, paunchiest, gobbiest, piggiest, of the 2 enforcers—Mutt, one of the killers Rack had warned were on the St. Louis crew—knows my rep and coughs up everything I want from him after I stick a bradawl through the webbed skin between his big toe and middle toe.

I educate him on the curriculum of pain he's about to learn, a curriculum starting from his feet and working its way up his body with various teaching aids from my heavy grip.

While Rack's in the bathroom trying to make himself pretty, I drag Mutt, who I guess is the boss of his 2-man hit squad, across the floor and into 'my bedroom'. My strategy is that I'll fuck the senior guy up a little, come outta the bedroom with a bloodstained tool in hand, and then get the junior guy, Yo-Yo (stupid fucking nickname), to spill all he knows outta fear of receiving the same treatment as his partner.

Don't need to. Turns out the senior hitter only likes inflicting pain and can't take a friendly lick from a runt Chihuahua let alone a couple of warmup digs, not even for the sake of professional pride.

I roll him onto the bed. I ain't worried about the mess I intend to make—it ain't my place.

"I'm leaving the tape on your mouth until I get your attention and you're ready to talk," I explain; "I'm gonna get my grip... gimme a sec."

Grip collected and tools back inside, I return and shut the door.

"Alright. You've probably guessed that my name ain't Logan. It don't really matter what it is, only that I'm known for this type of thing. My AKA's Halo if that means anything to you," I take a look at him while I rummage for my bradawl—a woodworking hand tool with a wood handle and a spiked blade similar to a stunted ice picker—and clock his eyes go wide with recognition, not at the tool, at the known byname I use; "What's gonna happen is, I'm gonna work you over until I find a motivating level of pain and then I'm gonna ask some questions, increasing the pain level if I feel your answers are less than forthcoming. Nod if you get me?"

He nods.

With the same knife I used to free Rack, I cut the lace on 1 shoe, the right 1, and pull it off followed by the sock. Mutt struggles, trying to escape from the inevitable. He's trussed up with nowhere to go. I seize an ankle and force the pick blade into webbed flesh. The bradawl needs a couple of hard twists to punch through, but the result's satisfyingly definitive. Gagged, crying, and garbled pleas are mumbled incoherently behind the duct tape. The paunchy crybaby is bouncing his whole body on the mattress springs. Frantic eyes and nodding head are attention seeking, he's desperate to talk—already?

I peel the tape away, the adhesive, not Hollywood movie fake tape low-tack glue, but adhesive designed to hold ducts together, pulls his pale and sweaty features outta shape, a final rip snaps his lips and cheeks back into place—I wax a patch of Brillo whiskers as a bonus.

"I'll talk. Anything you want, just stop!"

I'm as surprised as...

"Your name?"

"Mutt..."

"Real name?"

"Paul Sallazzo."

Sallazzo's keen to spill his guts with only a minor level of incentive, if I had an hour, he'd be my bitch, not that I'd actually douche the ugly cunt-faced snide, but he'd turn sis rather than endure borderline torture. In both our minds, I think we believed he was made of sterner stuff than the soft turd he turned out to be when the true stink of my negotiating methods caught in his nostrils.

"The other guy?"

"Yo-Yo... Leraci," sweat's pouring off his clammy forehead and stinging his piggy eyes. He rapid eye blinks, though he ain't REM dreaming this nightmare.

"You here for Rack or me or both?"

"Both."

"Your orders?"

I ask the easy questions 1st; questions that don't matter much, questions I can guess without much imagination.

"We were 'sposed to get you both together when Rack came back to the casino, but you did a runner, so we brought him back here and waited to see if you'd show."

"For a quiet chat, was it?"

Sallazzo's more reluctant now, he don't wanna admit to whatever depravity they had in store for Rack and me.

"Speak up or I pick another tool from the grip and see what else I can 'fix'... maybe a knee?"

"We were meant to find out why you was here and who sent you."

"Well, you'd be shit outta luck on that score. I work through a go-between, so I don't know nothing about the hire other than the specifics of the job," I knew more now than I did at the off, courtesy of my last call with Duke, but I ain't letting on to no 1 about that; "What happens when you can't get what you want outta me?"

Sallazzo shrugs—he don't wanna upset me further, I guess—but we both know I was destined for a crib hole in the ground and a quicklime blanket.

"Alright, the $10-million question, who the fuck wants me dead? Come on, Sallazzo, don't be shy. If you get this 1 right, you'll be able to walk outta here with all your toes."

I don't know if he believes me, but the promise of amputation-less freedom lubricates Sallazzo's snitch mechanism, and adrenaline is the fuel that keeps his motormouth running.

"C-Note sent us."

As overseer for the St. Louis investment, that was no surprise, but I gotta be thorough, "On Tricky's say so?"

A shake of the head.

"He knows, but C-Note's taking over the St. Louis operation and shorting the syndicate... Tricky works for him."

"But they're in it together?"

"C-Note's the hustle, Tricky holds the stake. They need each other if war breaks out."

"If or when?"

He shrugs. St. Louis' moves to break away are aggressive as would be Chicago's countermoves—blood would flow.

Now things are making more sense. Dave Fortuna's the brawn and the balls behind the hostile takeover. He ain't Tricky's handler, he's his senior partner, a made guy charged with keeping an eye on operations south of Chicago while 1 eye scans for opportunities profiting his maneuvers for power. Whether the takeover is exclusively local, or St. Louis has silent partners north of state who'll back a deal that'll minimize disruption to the casino operation whilst handing control over to C-Note and Tricky, who knew? Certainly not me, and undoubtedly not a low-ranker like Mutt.

"What else?"

"The bodyguards that keep Tricky safe report to C-Note, his thumb's jammed into Tricky's ass and his fingers are in the syndicate pie," he further enlightens, leaving me with a mental image that turns me off pie for the foreseeable.

"How's C-Note funding his takeover? Skimming the casino take sets him up, but a couple of mil bankroll won't last long on the streets if he plans to hustle large."

"Drugs, prostitution, illegal gambling, heists, chop shops, I know about, but that's just the tip. I don't know about the other stuff he's got going. Yo-Yo and me get orders to lean on this guy or that guy, keep the street rats in line, that's it."

"Come on, there's gotta be something else? C-Note and Tricky don't need to create this much friction. From what I hear, C-Note can hustle large as a sideline without fucking around with the status quo… what's really going on here?"

"The casino's fucked."

"What?"

"I don't know all the details, but it's built on contaminated ground: chemicals and toxic shit in the soil. Tricky got wind and paid off someone in the Building Division's examiner's office to bury the report. When C-Note found out, he took over. He don't know how long he can keep it under wraps, so he's setting himself up down here before the take runs dry."

"Is the city planning to condemn *The Furlough*?"

"And reclassify the land as a no-build zone. They'll have to tear the place down and decontaminate the soil before it's passed safe. It'll cost millions to meet building regs, and millions more in lost profits."

"You know this how?"

"I hand an envelope to the guy in the examiner's office once a month."

"Who's the guy?"

"In the examiner's office?"

"Are you fucking with me?" I wield the bradawl.

"No, no, his name's Gary Dursley."

"OK," I make a mental note; "If C-Note and Tricky do nothing, both get demoted back to the low-level grind?"

"Without the casino, C-Note's back to street hustling, and Tricky's outta the syndicate."

"Out?"

"He's a punk. Chicago bosses turn a blind eye on how he browns his dick when he's making green, but he's a jumped-up professional gambler they use to run the place and take the heat if the Feds audit the floor... without the casino, he's outta the high stakes game and spreading his bets with regular Joe punter.

"C-Note's the real shark swimming here, he's using Tricky just as much as Chicago is?"

"For a homo, Tricky's a mean bastard when he's got the upper hand or snorting coke, but he's a scared little bitch when a top dog like C-Note's pissing on his post."

"Plenty of scared little bitches around St. Louis," I insult; "I'm gonna have a word with Rack. He's probably gonna give you a dig or 2 for breaking his nose, but then we'll pack up and fuck off and you can limp back to C-Note and explain how you fucked this up."

"No hard feelings, yeah? You know the deal, it was business, nothing personal."

"That's how I feel about it too... *ummm*," I press my lips together to mime pressing lips together, signaling that Sallazzo oughta do the same so I can tape shut the gush of verbal diarrhea spurting from his asshole mouth.

# 15.

Rack might not be a Chicago club member, but he's Chicago bought and I'm freelance, our agendas are different, but our objective's the same—maybe. I'm almost certain that Rack was setup to bring this conflict of interests to a head and I was brought in to lance the boil when it didn't pop from his poking around. Like queers, the syndicate don't promote smokes into their ranks unless they're an asset of some kind and then they get connected, an affiliate of sorts, a guy but not a made guy.

I got nothing against the black man if he don't roll like a corner boy street nigger, and Rack walks like 1 of us. That being the case, I'm hoping he and me can come to an arrangement and not sweep each other 6 feet under the rug to tidy up this mess.

"Those motherfuckers," he's pissed.

"Fair."

"I oughta put a bullet in the back of their double-crossing skulls."

"I feel you," I don't point out the hypocrisy behind his double-crossing conclusion, everyone is playing everyone here, "but the smart thing would be to put some miles between; wait for the storm to blow over and see how the wind turns."

"Run and hide?"

"Run and live. Chicago's playing this as underhand as St. Louis," I also don't mention 'Mr. Black', Rack ain't earned that level of trust;

"Nobody wants to declare all-out war; the price is too great. But lines have been crossed and men have been marked and you and me have been left swinging in the whirlwind."

"Motherfuckers."

"D'you got fake ID? A cover nobody else knows?"

"Yeah, but I only got enough beans to feed me for a couple of months."

"Yeah, I'm gonna go hungry too. Might have to get a regular job."

"Motherfuckers."

"Like I said, that's the smart thing."

"Sounds like you got a dumb thing you wanna discuss?"

"Dumb as fuck."

"Let me hear it."

"We expose C-Note and Tricky: putting them in the crosshairs'll give us a minute without looking over our shoulders. Then we give Chicago the bad news about the casino, give up the payoff guy in the Building Division, give up what we know about St. Louis going it alone, then stand back so they can deal with their own and get back to barebacking profits from the casino like a nasty whore shitting out jizz enemas.

"Nice image."

"I've heard worse."

"Will it work?"

I shrug. I'm angry, and angry people make angry decisions, "Don't know. If we bust C-Note and Tricky, get them to cough up the stolen green, we got more to negotiate with than our word against theirs. Both greedy bastards'll have a personal stash with enough gas money to make Mexico if we can't get at the principal skim. Plus, I owe that tassel-shoe-wearing motherfucker a dig."

What I really need at this point is somebody to talk me outta my plan instead of going along with it—'cause 2 wrongs don't make it right—but Rack's skiing downslope and I'm riding the sled of premeditated payback.

"C-Note'll be hard to break. Tricky's got 2 guys covering his back, and the casino has banks of cameras and a shit load of witnesses."

"Fair. We concentrate on C-note, then," I check my Rolex; "He won't be at the casino yet, d'you know where he lives?"

"Yeah, I got that address."

"OK. They think I'm on the lam and you're being rolled in a rug. Chicago ain't ready to make a move and C-Note reckons he's on top of the situation. I think there's room to make some moves here."

"What d'you got in mind?"

"Get Mutt to call C-Note and confirm our demise and disappearance. Drive out to his place for an unfriendly visit and take his stash. If we're gonna get killed over this, might as well be at the front facing the enemy than taking a sniper round behind the ear hiding in the rear."

Cogs turn, options are weighed, risk vs reward is calculated.

For the 1st time in the short time I'd known him, Rack smiles, holds out a fist for me to bump, he's all in, "Yeah," he grins.

# 16.

I follow Rack in my Kia, he's driving the hitters' Lexus LS500, a nice car if you're making bank, and C-Note's hit squad, riding in the trunk, must be cash fluid under his management. They're dead now. As dead as we'd be if the situation was reversed; as dead as we still might be in a couple of hours if we misstep; or as dead as the motherfuckers on Rack and my shit list would be if shit goes sideways. The risk vs reward was still marginally a better prospect than the thought of stacking crates in a 'Nowheresville' warehouse on minimum wage while the dust settles. The trouble with gangsters is that they never forget, and a grudge lingers like a fart in an elevator, so the stink might cling to us unless I undo something to deodorize the unwelcome smell.

I force Mutt to make a call to C-Note informing their boss that I'd turned up at the apartment and Rack and me had been faded, and that they were getting rid of any trace that we'd ever existed. I warn Mutt not to slip in a euphemism or code word that'll tip his boss off to the fact that we're very much alive and very much pissed.

"Get this right and it gives us a few hours grace to move on. I'll phone the building manager to come and set you free when we're outta state," I convince Mutt, his partner, Yo-Yo, has been trussed up and gagged all this time.

Mutt does as is asked, answers all of my questions, and then I murder him by suffocation with a plastic bag over the head sealed tight with a zip-tie. I do the same for his backup man after Rack gives him a dig or 2. Suffocation leaves relatively little trace evidence at the scene of crime as long as you move the bodies soon afterward. We spend the next hour prepping our weapons cache, recharging the taser, making ready the hitters 9s, changing into raid clothing, and mummifying the dead in bed linen and duct tape until the tape runs out. I'd have to visit another hardware store to replenish. For right now, though, I got sufficient hardware to do it myself.

# 17.

Florissant, a mainly white middle-class northern suburb, is a half-hour drive from Central West End St. Louis. C-Note rents a half-brick, half-timber siding house on Fleur De Bois Drive. The property's set back from the road amid a secluded tree line at the end of a paved driveway. It's detached. Sufficiently isolated that noise won't be a problem if I gotta make someone scream.

I check the time on my TAG, my newest timepiece—3.28pm. It's sufficiently early that C-Note's probably still in his slippers, early enough that Tricky won't expect him for a few hours at least. I park the Kia in a gravel layby just up from the house and hop into the Lexus with Rack, my leather grip on the backseat.

We look at each other, dark clothing, baseball caps, bandanas pulled over our faces so only our eyes show—yeah, we look G.

"Set?"

"Ready."

"Go," I urge.

Rack grins, he's running on cocaine and retribution. An intoxicating mix that undoubtedly inspires his adoption of my plan, an intoxicating mix that might prove problematic. I get the impression that steroids and iron are a substitute for the drugs and mayhem Rack was into before his rehabilitation from volatile thug to reliable muscle took place. So long as he don't go on a rampage bender until after business is concluded, we'd be good.

Rack wheels onto the driveway of a, what has to be, 15-room house with attached garage. I take a quick scan, looking for CCTV and doorbell cameras, I don't spot any video capture security—maybe 'cause it's a rented house? Rack parks out front at an angle that obscures the driver and rider from view. As expected, C-Note sees the hitters' car pull up and storms out of the house to find out what the fuck's going on.

"What the fuck's going on?" he rages at the occupants, approaching the driver's side, only spotting the black seat cover when he's maybe 12 - 15 feet from his front porch.

It's plenty distance for me to swing the rider's side door and get a bead on him running back toward the house and presumably an anti-trespass device. He ain't stopping, so I shoot a leg out from under him. It takes 3 silenced *chuutes* for me to nick him without perforating something vital—he falls like a sack of bowel cancer shit, spilling blood all over the driveway.

Rack and me get a *'D'you know who you're fucking with?'* earache when we drag his shot ass through the front door. Just inside the hall C-Note's cliché wife, dressed in a throwback red pantsuit and house slippers, appears to find out what all the commotion's about. I slap her with the 9s muzzle, sending her to the floor with a yelp. Another whack to the back of her bottle-blonde skull with the butt cuts the shrieking off—she slumps as only a KO'd person can, limp as a geriatric dick.

*"You fucking cocksuckers!"* C-Note rages harder than before, he must really love his wife, at least more than the hookers who drain his prick at the casino, and that's a hook I can reel this shark in with.

"Anyone else in the house? Kids, maid, dogs, anyone?"

He knows the score. If I find out he's trying to hide something or somebody from me then the violence will be shared around, especially if some slobbering Great Dane tries to take a bite outta my ass.

"No... no dogs, kids at college, maid's gone for the day."

"What about cameras?"

"Security systems off."

I check again, for cameras and PIR sensor lights—nada.

The whole ground floor's walk-through open plan other than 1 door off the entrance hall I assume ain't the shitter.

"Take him in there. I'm gonna tidy things out here," I point the 9 at the door, Rack drags C-Note towards it, leave a bloody trail across the marble tile.

"Don't hurt my wife," C-Note warns, but his influence over our actions has melted away like ice on a summer's day.

I shut the front door on the civilized world and any nosey neighbors and pull the wife deeper into the hallway, zip-tying her wrists and ankles. She sports a red cheek and swollen eye where she fell heavy to the floor, scalp blood mixes with her block-color dye job—she's out cold.

Behind the hallway door is a study cum office. C-Note likes his impressive desks; he has the same lump of oak installed in his casino office as installed at home. Sitting behind 1 must fill him with an overblown sense of importance. Of course, he's also filling the mouths of kneeling hookers in the kneehole of his casino desk while his wife's in the kitchen at home making lasagna to fill his mouth when he's done fucking with people's lives for the day.

I the room check out.

Along 1 wall of the study is a bookcase full of classic literature. I don't take C-Note for a Shakespearean scholar, he's more your Playboy subscriber—for the articles—so I take an educated guess that there's a safe hidden behind. In the center of the west-facing wall is a window looking out onto a side lawn and discreet tree line separating this property from the immediate righthand neighbor. The rest is as you'd expect a faux turn of the last century study to be decorated: maps on the wall, drinks cabinet, couple of reading chairs, portentous shit like that—I don't see any cameras.

When I'm certain there ain't no electronic eyeballs watching my every move, I squat so that C-note and me are eye level with each other, "Behind the bookcase, is it?"

"Fuck you, you dumb cunt!" he ain't to happy.

I pull the bandana down, "My name's Halo," yeah, he'd heard of my reputation; "This whole thing's fucked. I know who you are, but you can't threaten a man you already put a contract out on, you dumb cunt. Somebody's gotta pay for putting my name on a hit list. Those fucktards you sent after Rack and me got theirs and now it's your turn. We need to disappear and you're gonna divvy up for our unplanned vacations... consider it compensation and out-of-pocket expenses," I try on.

"What am I, born yesterday? As soon as you open the safe, I'm a dead man. You can't leave me alive and expect me to forgive what you done to my wife. You're getting nothing outta me. At least I'll die knowing you 2 cunts are on the lam with nothing but lint in your pockets."

"There's that nasty word again. What d'you think about being called the c-word by C-Note, Rack?"

"I don't like."

I push down on the hole in his leg with the silencer muzzle and receive a satisfying hiss through C-Note's gritted teeth. Our plan's to pass on what we got to Chicago and let them fix the leak; but our host don't know that, he thinks this is a straight-up heist.

"You know I brought my tool grip with me," I caution, but C-Note stays G. I'd have to get dental on this hard case before he'd feed me a bullshit answer, and practically medieval before he'd give up the truth.

"Do what you like. It'll take hours you don't got to make me talk. Tricky's expecting me at the casino, he'll send some soldiers to check up on the house when I'm a no show and he can't get hold of me. You and Rack are burned."

That was bullshit. I can smell the lie on his breath.

1st off, it won't take hours to get something outta him, and 2nd, Tricky ain't expecting him anytime soon, but C-Note's mind was set to make me work for everything I got.

"I ain't thinking about tooling down on you," I threaten; "But your wife?"

"Hey, she's a civilian..."

"...she's collateral damage," I cut him off; "Like you said, we don't got time to piss about."

C-Note goes pale. Admittedly he's losing blood, but I can tell I'd hit a nerve of a different kind. Time to turn the screws.

"What's your wife's name?"

He don't wanna answer, but it ain't worth the pain of holding out on that information, "Maura."

"I'm gonna get my grip from the car. It'll take a couple of minutes for me to choose something... persuasive... pliers maybe. I think Maura'll tell me anything I wanna know after I rip her painted toenails out. In the meantime, Rack's gonna fuck her in the ass and then in the mouth to loosen her up."

That was the straw.

The back of C-Note's resistance breaks at the idea of a big black cock railing Mrs. Fortuna butt to mouth—some waps are funny that way.

"940818."

"Anniversary?"

C-Note nods.

"Sweet."

"You'll need my thumbprint as well," he gives up.

"Do I got to use bolt cutters or are you gonna give us a thumbs up?"

"My wife?"

"The maid comes in the morning?"

He nods.

"We'll lock Maura in a closet or something with some water."

"No need for a bolt cutter, I'll do it."

"Bussin" Rack approves.

As I guessed, the mid-section of the bookcase swings out on a hinge and a decent-sized safe with an electronic keypad and biometric lock is revealed. Rack holds C-Note up while I punch in his anniversary digits and then get him to scan his thumb digit. We hear the rewarding clunk of a lock mechanism opening and the safe door pops.

"Now your phone."

"What?"

"There ain't enough room for 4-mil in cash in there. But you might got enough online bank to pay us off and pay back what you owe Chicago from your offshore accounts. If we close this deal in profit, maybe I'll tie a tourniquet 'round your leg and put you in the closet with your wife?"

"I don't have the money."

I give him a skeptical look.

"Not personally. It's stashed at the casino, in the penthouse safe installed for high-rollers."

It's more bullshit, he's saving his savings for his widow's pension, "How much?"

"Last count... 6-mil."

That hard 6 meant there was at least another 6 working the angles and streets.

"Fuck, that's a lot of juice," Rack licks his lips, he's hungry for his greens.

"Business is good. You speculate you accumulate," C-Note brags, his tone ironic considering that business was about to get bad, real bad.

"It'll be better if we check your online credit 1st."

"Better for you or for me?"

"Better for your wife."

"My stash sits with a broker... even I can't get it the same day."

"The fuck you say," Rack leans over C-Note, he ain't buying it.

"D'you know how much petty cash I get running a casino? I don't need money in my pocket or a bank account, my bank's tied up in stocks and shares. Go shakedown the stock exchange if you want my money, 'cause I got what's in my wallet and that's it. Now take what's in the safe and *get the fuck outta my house!*"

I think about it; think about the 2 safes; think about all that petty cash; think up a revised plan.

"The penthouse safe... Tricky's got access?"

For all his entitled bravado and inflated bluster, C-Note visibly sags, he's G enough to know what's coming next, "Yeah... make it quick."

A rewarding clunk of the 9's mechanism, simultaneous with a silenced *chuute* of ballistic propellent, pops a bullet through C-Note's skull—the heavy round buries itself in his preposterous oak desk, scattering frothy brain and red blood and bone fragments, along with his right eyeball, across the varnished side panel.

"Fuuuck?" Rack steps back, the devil in me just made the room we're in hotter than hell and my partner in crime is sweating cobs.

"He had it coming," my anger is cool, but icing C-Note, however good it feels in the moment, is pure indulgence; "Let's get what we're owed."

Rack and me are blood brothers now, but we still don't trust each other enough for 1 of us to find a lockable room to secure Maura in until morning while the other empties the safe of its contents.

Some jewelry: diamond baubles and ruby whatnots. Rolexes, his and hers, gold. If the gent's watch was an Omega, I might have tossed a coin for it. As it ain't, I give them both to Rack. Passports, documents, a pair of double-cross double-entry ledgers I keep as a bargaining tool. C-Note was old-school, I would've used an encrypted thumb drive or even a secure cloud to store sensitive, incriminating, information like this, but he did use the precaution of a gobbledygook code of acronyms and hieroglyphs that I can't make sense outta.

There's 40-liters of gas money I split 50/50. I cut out for myself some jewelry equivalent to what I reckon the watches are worth. Divide the rest of the necklaces, bracelets, rings, and earrings into 2 piles, palming a nice pair of diamond earrings and matching bracelet like a close-in magician at a Vagas lounge show. Honor amongst thieves only stretches so far, and I'm a criminal who's just slotted 3 Gs and pistol-whipped a woman unconscious, so I'm due a bonus.

There's a zip of coke in there too, I leave it on the desk and Rack takes it along with the shit I'd split with him. He doesn't complain, it's sufficient capital to run for a while, sufficient for a year, at least, but the coke ain't gonna last that long. He's bumping some more blow and stuffing his share of the safe haul into a briefcase he finds under the desk as I go through the drawers and find car keys to a Mercedes, presumably parked inside the attached garage. We can't touch it, let alone drive it away from the house, we're trying to dump evidence not collect more shit. Rack'll have to ride along with me in the Kia—wherever that destination might be.

I throw the car keys back in the drawer but take a nice-looking gold lighter. In another drawer, I find what I'm looking for: a black VIP keycard with *The Furlough* embossed in gold across its face. I hold it up for Rack to see.

"We'll leave the Lexus with the dead weight in the trunk for the cops. We've got enough cash and valuables to fence, and the ledgers might keep Chicago off our backs for cooling their guy, but we can't ever come back, Illinois is death to us. Even if C-Note was shorting the big boys and planning on moving out on his own with their money, he was still a club member, so we're persona non grata," I run down but don't apologize for snuffing C-Note, we were fucked from the start of this thing; "Decision time: we take what we got and go do something else somewhere else as someone else, or we try on a deal with Chicago, or we go for broke, get Tricky to open the penthouse safe and maybe recover enough money before he finds out his ex-partner can't back him from the grave and does a runner with the skim. Along with the ledgers and the name of the building inspector C-Note's paying off to keep the casino from being pulled down, we got a decent shot at buying ourselves outta trouble with the boys up north?"

The main casino vault was way, way off limits. We'd never get past the professional security arrangements, the armed guards, the alarms, and make our escape without either getting shot, locked behind a security door, or felt up by the cops. Plus, that money was 95% legit bank for the syndicate, touch it and no amount of restitution would secure their forgiveness.

"Well, you just shot my credit with Chicago to shit... what the hell, might as well go all-in for the best deal."

"Fair. We can't snuff Tricky, though. We oughta leave someone for the syndicate to take their anger out on."

"Smart."

"Alright, let's throw C-Note's old lady in a closet and take a drive back into town. By the way, I'm taking the humidor for myself. If we get outta this alive, I'm celebrating with a Cuban cigar," and an outta sight, outta mind Thai vacation, but I keep that part of my exit strategy strictly between me and my travel broker.

"Cool… could you stake me a smoke? I'm gonna celebrate with a fat 1 when this is over," he grins, his nostrils full of party powder.

"You got it, brother," I pat his bulky shoulder, it's good to have a partner. Especially, a wide partner I can dodge behind if bullets start to fly.

I leave C-Note's pinky ring on it's finger, he stayed G until the end—that's something to respect.

# 18.

Nobody recognized the Kia. Why would they, its appearance at the casino is virgin. We swipe into the employee parking lot using C-Note's keycard and find a parking space removed from the other parked cars. When I bought the Kia, I'd made sure that the license plates contained black numbers and letters, that way a strip of black electrical tape can turn Ps into Rs and 3s into Bs and 1s and Is into Ts or Ls, voiding the ability of license plate recognition cameras and CCTV footage from following my movements when I need a quick cover vehicle. It's a simple hack that don't involve screwdrivers and rounded-off screws and false plates, yet fools automated tracking systems and eyewitness statements, passing all but the closest visual inspection.

I'd changed up a few numerals before we headed out. Threw my personal effects in the trunk, added the cash and valuables we'd looted from C-Note's safe stuffed into a garbage bag, included the incriminating ledgers I'm confident are worth some measure of bargaining.

As the sun sinks into evening, night creeps up on the world like a cold shadow at my back. Most of *The Furlough's* employees are at their respective stations, working the countless jobs required to run a busy casino. As usual, the smokers and the loafers are hanging outside for a sneaky break or sat in their cars scrolling Instagram, TikTok, Twitter, or whatever—their faces lit by cell phone displays they don't look up from when we pass. Me, with my leather grip in hand and baseball cap on my head. Rack, with a 9 tucked into his waistband under a black jacket and a baseball cap slightly on the hip-hop skew.

I recall the route we took last time: through a network of corridors and service elevators to the admin floor, exiting into the corridor where C-Note has a 2nd oak desk set up in his now obsolete 2nd office.

Unless they seal the room up with him entombed inside like a casino pharaoh—more appropriate for the pyramid *Luxor Hotel and Casino* on the Las Vegas strip than St. Louis—another syndicated guy will be getting his knob polished under the desk by Lexi in a few days. At the end of the corridor, recessed into a gold effect doorframe cut into the wall, a pair of gold-faced sliding doors leading to the penthouse level elevator are firmly shut. No 1 else is around when I call the elevator with a swipe of the black keycard, waiting for it to descend next to an increasingly nervous Rack.

"You, OK?" I ask, stretching black gloves over my hands.

He eyes me with dilated pupils, "Yeah. It's been a minute since I got high. I forgot how many gears coke gives you. I'm revving, brother."

"Take it easy when we get up there," I caution, wriggling my fingers to get my gloves to fit… like a glove.

"Don't worry 'bout me, I'm golden," he blinks, his swollen eye sheds a tear that runs down his cheek.

I hear the elevator car mechanism whirr to our floor, hear a ping, then the doors open. A 9s tucked under my jacket, a blue off-the-peg number borrowed from C-Note's walk-in closet when we locked his wife in there, so I'd fit in with the casino's semi-formal attired crowd. I hadn't collected the jacket I stashed under a dumpster last night, some street person at The Grove is probably breaking it in by now. My chest's too big to button up the jacket front, and my arms too long for the cuff to cover my Tag Heuer. It don't matter, this ain't a fashion show, and I ain't a model civilian. My hard-hitting reputation is my style, not the threads I wear or the car I drive or the women I fuck or the watch I tell time by.

Rack takes the taser from his jacket side pocket and holds it poised to jolt. I don't got to draw a weapon; the elevator car is empty. I feel a few nerves when I press the button to take us to the top floor. There are only 4 buttons to choose from on the operating panel: (P) for penthouse – (A) for Admin floor, where we got on – (CF) for casino floor – (G) for the garage level. Going over the plan earlier, Rack explains that the floors this elevator services are unobserved by security or cameras, but the garage is a forbidden realm attended and operated by a security guard and valet, and strictly off-limits for those without executive permission—even C-note's swipe can't bypass that security arrangement. So, the route we take through the casino is the least conspicuous route to gain the upper level.

10 seconds, no more, of the smoothest elevator ride I'd ever taken. It's ample time to ready ourselves and our weapons—I screw a silencer onto the muzzle of my gun. The grip feels heavy in my hand.

I raise the 9 I'd shot C-Note with as soon as the doors open onto deep-pile carpet swathing a deep red corridor full of waiting goons.

The taser in my spine sinks me to 1 knee, but I'm strong enough to send Rack's nuts deep into his abdomen with a rearward uppercut elbow. The double-triple-crossing motherfucker drops faster than I do, and then the world goes crazy for 2 - 3 seconds as Tricky's personal security team sends my vision to the stars and then my consciousness into darkness.

# 19.

I'm hurt. My eyes are closed. 1 of them from tightness and pain that can only be a bruise of proper significance. I don't know what hit me, but my orbital bone throbs deep enough to be fractured. The ribs on my right side are sore, but I can mouth-breathe OK. I won't be taking any breaths through my nose without sounding like I'm sucking milkshake dregs through a straw until I can thumb out a wad clotting blood, and that would be a problem as both hands, stripped of gloves and fingerprint naked, are zip-tied to the back of a reproduction antique wooden chair. My ankles are similarly secured to the chair's legs, I'm hatless, but they left my shoes and socks on.

I'd been caught.

I'd been floored.

I'd been out.

This is it. I'm about to get what I'd been doing to others for a decade and what Mutt and Yo-Yo intended to do to me before I'd bagged their heads like fairground goldfish. I'm the fish now, trapped with the prospect of hard questioning and harder pain to inspire a straight flow of answers. I wonder how long I can hold out. I wonder if resistance for the sake of pride is worth the misery I'd suffer before the final question is asked and the final answer given, and a coked-up Rack takes revenge for what I've done to his chances of fatherhood.

I wonder about this while faking unconsciousness, stealing an extra minute to collect what sense I got in my numbskull before the dim idea to break and enter a gangster's house to rip-off his stash transitioned into raiding the penthouse safe of a St. Louis casino. Sure as shit, God ain't gonna answer any prayer I send His way to save my dirty soul. My madly religious mother ruined the Faith for me, and then I'd stuck a finger up to God's hypocrisy, so I whisper a curse for the Devil and accept that black fate has darkened the fortune of unsaintly Saint Greaves.

Water!

It splashes me into an involuntary response.

"Wakey, wakey, Mr. Anthony," It's Tricky leaning over me, his bitch boyfriend at his side twitching with ADHD excitement; "Not your real name we can presume;" he's holding my fake ID, taken from me when they patted me down for weapons and cell phone. I ain't green enough to carry a cell into this situation, not that it has many contacts stored. He throws the ID contemptuously across the vault floor.

My good eye—the right—scans my surroundings. I'm inside the penthouse walk-in safe. Fuck, it's crammed with cash, more than I'd ever seen in my life, and more than I'd ever see again in the shortening hours or minutes left to me. I take a guess at the reason behind my current location: they don't wanna get the plush décor and carpeting in the penthouse living space gouted with gore.

Tricky's flexing hard, waving a big-shot handgun that shines like a *sureños ese's* tricked-out *pistola*. Maybe he'd been given the spiced-up M1911 Colt as a goodwill gesture by the cartel for buying into the St. Louis drug market. Maybe he just likes shiny shit?

"Rack tells me you go by Halo. I asked around about a hitter using that name and..." he smacks the Colt's barrel slide into the palm of his left hand, the gesture signifying instant gratification. Rack overheard me threatening C-Note with my AKA reputation just before I emptied the syndicate boss's head of all vindictive thoughts concerning yours truly—he's ratted me out good, "...just like that, my sources tell me you have a notorious rep as a small-time debt collector and muscle for hire. You're not that bright, but you get the job done through brute force and determination. An excellent trait in your line, but sadly lacking when you try and fail to step up into the big leagues.

I know you were contracted to nose around and find out about the discrepancy in profits my dearly departed partner and I were redirecting into other business opportunities. What I don't know, is who sent you? Rack was passed instructions through a 3rd or 4th party connected to the Chicago club, but he's on my team now. You, however, you're not on anyone's team but your own... You were contracted through middlemen the same as Rack, but you might know something he doesn't, so we're going to ask some pointed questions?" he didn't ask, he just kept talking; "As you can imagine, Rack is seriously pissed at the blow you dealt his black, and now black and blue, balls. He wants to do the questioning, but I'm going to give you a chance, 1 chance to tell me what I want to know so we don't have to draw this ordeal out. Not that we're at your level of expertise, but we do have your goodie bag of tools to choose from," he indicates 1 of the 3 wall-to-ceiling stainless steel shelving units where my grip is resting on a middle shelf. The other 2 units are resting wads of banded money.

I guess the zip-ties around my wrists and ankles, as well as the implements of DIY torture about to be used on me, are my own. That pisses me off more than my impending torture and motivates my anti-pussying-out ego into forcing my captors to roll up their sleeves and get to work.

"Don't any of you motherless cocksuckers have your own shit to work a guy over with?" I question; "Mutt and Yo-Yo already cost me 5 bucks in cable-ties," I estimate, my lips and teeth not yet distorted or broken, so I'm coherent enough for the glib counter to sound stoic.

"Send me the bill and I'll cover the cost. Now, who hired you to come into my yard and start a riot?"

"I ain't saying shit."

"If you don't know, give me the name of your contact and you can pass the hurt onto them."

"Better get a mop and bucket ready, 'cause this floor's gonna need washing down if you ever stop fucking talking and start doing."

"I don't have anything else to add, other than you did me a favor ex-ing Fortuna. Once I take what information you think you can keep from me, I can lay the blame on him and you, and Rack'll back me up. Play my cards right and I'll be king on a golden throne by the time the casino folds."

King. More like queen, I think.

Rack. He must have got the idea to set this up with Tricky when I was sweet-talking C-Note's not-so-tough guy back at the apartment. He'd had 30-minutes driving the goons' Lexus from his place to Florissant to talk through arrangements with his new employer—cell phones, they get more people killed than guns.

Both of these motherfuckers owe me a debt of pain now, a debt I won't be able to collect, which angers me some more. I hold onto that anger, let it well up and soak me through—yeah, I'm gonna make them work for the nothing I had to tell them.

"I may not be as smart as the 2-timing hustler you think you are, but I'm fucking awesome at debt collecting and 2 other things: I'm awesome at fighting and holding out, and you've pissed me off enough I wanna prove I ain't bragging."

"Halo, you're awesome at pissing people off too, but not so fucking awesome at reading them," he hits me with a bitch slap that knocks the spit outta my mouth. I'd say Tricky has a boner for his flash pistola, and that inclination stops him whipping me about the head with it—small mercies, yeah.

I accept the slap as hors d'oeuvres and prepare for the main course, only it won't be Tricky or his pet rent boy, or 1 of his security goons dishing out the torture, it'll be my bad blood brother, Rack.

"Find out what you can. He's all yours," Tricky, the Queen of St. Louis, offers his new lacky a free hand.

Rack hobbles in. I wink at him with my good eye, he don't wink back with his.

"You got me good, Halo. Had to chill my balls with ice from the bar. Swelling's gonna last longer than you will," he warns; "I'd say you got a 1/2-hour max," he checks his watch to emphasize time running out—it's a Black bezel Tag Heuer.

"Hey, I only just got that watch."

"Mine now. When I finish up here, I'm gonna smoke 1 of your cigars and take the rest of your shit from the trunk of that shitty Kia, and then I'm gonna have it crushed with you inside," he gloats, searching through my bag and fitting Mutt's brass knuckles over the fingers of his left fist; "Torture's not my game. I do it when I gotta; and when I gotta, I prefer a more hands-on approach."

He rushes 2 steps and delivers a sickening brass-weighted punch just to the right of my liver. My bladder gets a tsunami of hurt flood through it. The pain's intense, but I can wear it. Even so, I decide to let the piss flow, it's my only way of fighting back.

Rack rushes 2 steps back to avoid the puddle, "What the fuck are you laughing at?" he demands.

"I told your boyfriend he'd need a mop and bucket to clean up in here before..."

I don't get to finish my verbal counter, another punch, this time a right hook to the right side, crushes my spleen even though I tense. That 1 hurt like a hit-and-run felony, and then my liver catches a left hook right on the money. I nearly crack a tooth gritting my teeth so hard.

I'm gasping for breath, making weird involuntary heaving, sobbing sounds until I get my breath back.

"Your employer's name or your go-between?"

I blow hard to clear the clotting obstruction in my nose, a bloody sneeze decorates my black tee, soaking into the material.

"I'm definitely gonna puke up my brunch if you keep going to the body, but I ain't puking up any names or shitting out anything you wanna smell in the foreseeable," I promise, which is a lie, everyone breaks at some point, and Rack ain't gotten revenge for his balls on mine yet. That would test my defiance, twice over.

Then he digs a piston straight right into my gut.

Projectile vomit prompts Rack to skip back through the safe door. His hasty retreat refreshes a wince of pain, reminding him of the testicular trauma I caused.

"I expected more from you, Grip."

"Really? I'm kinda proud of myself. I'm doing better than Mutt, Yo-Yo, and C-Note," I manage to gasp, it's a win of sorts, a tiny raft of defiance I cling to.

"You can sit there and enjoy the stink you've made and think over the choices you're not leaving me. I'm gonna take a bump. When I come back, I'm gonna shoot you in the good fellas," he means lefty and righty; "Then I'll ask for a name... *again.* If you give up what we want, I'll end it as quick as you did for C-Note, for old times' sake," he sneers; "Just 1 name and then..."

"...fucks sake, I'd rather take a headshot than listen to you whine on all night like a ragging bitch."

He shakes his lumpy head like he regrets the lead lap dance he just threatened to give my favorite testicles in the whole wide world. The ungrateful prick is in better shape than the dead serious treatment Mutt and Yo-Yo would've carried out on him under C-Note's orders if I hadn't saved his black ass. Should I expect more from a mercenary douchebag looking out for number 1? I should've known better.

Rack leaves me to mull my choices over, though, I got a decent grasp of what I can expect when he gets back to me, whether I hold out or not.

The safe door bangs shut, and the locking bolts engage. The interior space turns eerily silent, securing me inside a puke and piss-reeking room with no air. An LED strip light illuminates the interior. I can see millions in payoff monies and skim and not a $ would see the inside of my wallet. Not that I got a wallet: Rack has taken it, taken my watch, and taken the key to my Kia. So, his boast about smoking my cigars, and using my gas to drive my diamonds and gold baubles to the nearest fence ain't idle. I'd give every $100 bill on every shelf for 1/2 a chance, 1 fighting chance rather than no chance at all.

Ending up as a eunuch with onsetting knuckleduster-induced dementia and a Houdini appendix is gonna ruin an already crappy day—my last crappy day alive, as it happens. And then I see 1/2 a chance, a 1/4 of a chance, but a fraction of hope is all a fighter like me needs to come out for the final round swinging. The moronic, coked-up son of a ghetto whore has locked me in a soundproof safe with my leather grip.

# 20.

I'm in a state, wearing an undersized blue tracksuit and sneakers, bandaged in bedsheets, tuned up, tased, abrasions and bruises decorating my body, high on bleach fumes, with an entry and exit bullet wound throbbing on my right-side like a white-hot poker'd seared through that large, flat back muscle attached that stretches around the side behind the arm like a wing when you put it under tension. When I call Erika, I still have all my teeth, even my dental implant, so I sound coherent, if a little concussed, but not as concussed as I'd been in the casino safe. If I have a drop in mental acuity it's due to exhaustion rather than brain damage.

"Saint, is that you? You sound… different."

"Yeah, I got into a car crash, not my fault, but I'm a bit banged up."

"Oh my God, not another 1," she refers to the fictional accident that covered a false history of my battle-worn scar tissue and pugilist face; "Are you OK?"

"I'll live. Bumps and bruises, nothing broken, but I can't drive far."

"Are you still in St. Louis?"

"That's why I called… really out there ask: can I crash at yours tonight?"

"I mean, yes, of course. Are you in the emergency room? I can come pick you up?"

"Actually, I'm outside your place."

"In the street?"

"No, in my car."
"You drove? Is that safe?"
"Yeah, the damage is minor."
"I'm more worried about the damage to you than the car?"
"I won't lie, it's... uncomfortable. I'm gonna need some whiskey anesthetic. Can you bring a bottle from the bar, I got money to pay you back."
"I don't think you're supposed to drink if you're taking painkillers."
"Don't worry. I'm a practiced hand at pain control."
"If you're sure?" she don't sound too convinced.
"It'll take the edge off," and wash the taste of blood from inside my mouth.
"OooK? *Del!*" she calls the *Chromatic*'s bar manager over; "I need to go: a friend of mine has just been in a car accident," I overhear the explanation.
Del's sympathetic, "Go, we'll cover for you, Erik."
"I'll be home in 10 minutes."
"Don't break the speed limit or nothing, I don't want you getting pulled over on my account."
"See you soon, Saint. I'm sorry you had to stay in the city because of an accident, but I'm not sorry to hear from you again."
"Erika, you might be the only person in this world, let alone this city, pleased to hear from me today."
"See you soon."
"You bet."
The line goes dead. I make 1 more call and then oblivion hits me like a left hook from Tyson in his

prime and I black out like 1 of his victims... I mean opponents.

# 21.

72 hours ago, when the safe door cracked, I'm a heavily armed 200-odd-pound wedge at the gap ready to put my bodyweight between the 12-gauge steel doorframe and the 300-odd-pound out-swinging door. The frame height's too low to drop an arcing hammer onto my captors' heads, so I stab forward with a machete in my right fist, aiming for the 1st throat within reach, missing the target by inches as Rack tries to shield himself behind the door. Even so, I manage to separate his cheek from the bone.

He squeals, turns away from the blade instead of putting his counterweight into closing the door and I thread myself through the opening like an angry bull leaping from a rodeo chute gate. My horns are a ball peen hammer in my left hand and a machete in my right. My face is a Halloween mask of snot-clot blown from my nose and soft tissue swelling. The event riders are Rack and Tricky's 2 henchmen.

Instead of drawing heaters, the goons try to strongarm me—you can't get info from a dead man and Tricky wants me to talk. It's their undoing, 1 has a steel hammerhead smashed into his bonehead. My swing is violently efficient now that over head restriction's gone. The 2nd goon takes the machete blade across his outstretched hand, losing enough fingers that he'd never be able to count to 10 again without taking off his shoes and socks. I give him 2 more chops for luck. More fingers and an ear drop onto the carpet, and then I turn back to Rack who's got a silenced 9 pointing at me—I've inflicted enough hurt on him that he's gunning for me now.

I slip left with the machete raised to strike just as the muzzle flares and a suppressed discharge sends a hot projectile through my body. Without knowing how bad I'd been hit, I lash the blade down, ignoring the rip of white-hot pain and fear, severing Rack's hand at the wrist as another bullet explodes from the muzzle, smacking into the fingerless goon who's bent over failing to pick up his ear with his finger stumps. The 9 hits the plush deck with Rack's hand still holding onto the grip. Frenzied hacking and a front push kick sends the short-assed G to the floor, where I all but cleave his head in 2 with a fucking brutal chopping blow to the forehead that cuts a cleft palate through his mouth, severing our partnership for good.

"2-faced pigmy cunt," I spit at him, the literal overtone not lost on me.

Outta professorial solidarity, I wasn't gonna take any cheap shots at Rack's diminutive height. That was before he'd made me throw up my breakfast: the midget mobster.

I 9 up and check my corners. Hammerhead goon is down for the count, his brain pickled in blood brine, his breathing ragged. Fingers McEarloss is suffering shock from multiple slashes to his head and shoulders, multiple amputations, and Rack's wayward shot to the abdomen. I give him a bullet center of mass, then another, then 1 to the forehead. 1 for me and 4 for the goon leaves 3 rounds in the 9's single-stack clip.

The only exit is a door that opens to who knows where. I was unconscious when they dragged me into the safe and felt me up for weapons and ID, so I got no bearings. The small anteroom I'd just turned into a butchery is a windowless secure room, so I don't know which end of the building I'm at. The only good thing about my current situation is that this sealed area appears to be soundproofed.

I search the shot-to-shit dead guy for more ammo, he's got a Sig 9, so I stick another heater in my belt, same with the other goon, so I'm carrying 3 pistols charged with 21 bullets—that oughta light up anyone chunking jacketed lead my way.

I pull the fingerless goon outta the exit door's arc and open it a crack. A quick scan left and right, offering the smallest target possible, reveals the straight run elevator corridor. The corridor is a communication throughway with penthouse apartments spurring off on the other side from me and what looks like amenities and maintenance on my side. I know this because, the room doors opposite have names like the *Magenta Room* and the *Ivory Suite* instead of room numbers, and the door next to has a plaque that declares *Housekeeping.* I risk my shoulders and then 1 leg, noting that the next room down is a sauna. No 1's around, not surprising as this evening's liturgical penthouse entertainment is billed as Saint break Halo's balls Day.

Maximizing privacy, there ain't any cameras installed on this level, and there ain't 1 on or in the executive elevator either, so my presence is totally unrecorded. I guess that a 'Do Not Disturb' call has gone down to the lower-level staff, which means I got this floor to myself, other than Tricky and his squeeze, so I can revise the original plan, which now includes taking the money and shooting the remaining pair of cunts lefthanded. Lefthanded because it hurts like... well, like getting shot in the side, to lift my right arm. Now the adrenaline-fueled fight in the walk-in safe's anteroom is over, I feel every dig and wound like I've been used as a living voodoo doll.

I traipse down the central corridor, scanning left and right with my good eye, reaching the *Side Bet Lounge*. The entrance doors are glass, revealing a plush, very well-appointed, bar and small lounge for entertaining. Currently, the lounge is entertaining only 2 patrons who ain't drinking at the marble bar top, they're cutting lines and snorting stupidity from its polished surface.

With no VIP guestlist security on the door, I invite myself in. The sound system is blasting tunes from the last century—currently, Stevie Nicks' *Edge of Seventeen*. Tricky's toyboy is spinning a dance on the marble tiled floor running along the bar riser.

I never got his name, but he knows mine, *"Halo!"* he screeches, stopping mid-pirouette and pointing at my undesirable appearance; "Shoot him, Ricky!"

That ain't a nice welcome, nor is Ricky's scrabble to get to his flashy, nickel-plated *pistola*.

Tricky's Peg is dancing on the spot like he needs to piss, screaming hysterical instructions for his sugar daddy to introduce my body to high-velocity nudges—*fuck that*, I move my stationary target ass and start blazing.

Obviously, Tricky has never been downrange, 'cause he's a worse shot with his favored hand and 2 good eyes than I am shooting goofy with piss-poor depth perception—but only by a margin. The glass doors shatter behind me, the mirrored back wall and drinks shelf behind the bar explode into fragments. After all the mayhem and killing, hearing the nickel-plated .45 bark at me is a startling contrast to the phew, phew of the silenced 9 I'm wrecking the interior décor with.

I shut the shrieking pissant up with a stray jacketed NATO round, hitting him in the shoulder, spinning the dancing queen some more. Unlike my gunshot wound, the bullet strikes hard mass. GSWs to the shoulder ain't like you see in the movies, where the adult pretender brushes the injury off by coolly mentioning that the hole through his body has a clean exit and wears the pain with as much concern as a skinned knee. There's a lot of anatomy going on in the shoulder, most of it fucking up your ability to move the arm on that side if it gets hit—as my latest victim just found out—and there's some major get dead quick arteries road-mapping through that anatomical junction as well.

Tricky goes into full berserker mode after I clip his prick warmer, bellowing gun smoke and full metal jacket chaos.

Parabellum—prepare for war.

I blaze back, swapping 9s and slotting 2 into my opponent from the unsilenced Sig as his bullets buzz by my cauliflower ears within an inch of hitting the melon and spraying brain mucus out the back of my head. His gun clatters to the tiles, mine fires twice more and then goes click. No 1's dead, no 1 ain't shot, only 1 of us is crying, and it ain't Tricky or me.

"Sorry about your place, Tricky, hope you got insurance?" I wisecrack, gun smoke hanging in the air between us.

The mob boss wannabe crawls over to the mahogany bar riser and sits against the Swiss cheese bullet-holed panel, "We can make a deal," he offers, trying to stem the blood flow with compressing hands.

"Too late. I'm up to my neck and drowning, only 1 way to get back on dry land," I explain, crouching next to him.

"Fix me, fix your problem with Chicago?"

I nod, put the empty Sig on the floor, and pull Tricky's hand away from the hole in his chest. The music's too loud to hear the crackling-bubbling sound of a ruptured lung, but fluid in Tricky's bronchial tubes makes him cough like a Dickensian orphan.

"Will you let Jamie go?"

I guess Jamie's the name of his boyfriend. I shake my head. Jamie's a witness, a crybaby, and he asked his sugar daddy to shoot me—that's 3 strikes.

"I'll make it quick," is all I promise, taking the bling-bang from the floor and checking the chamber.

I don't know how many rounds Tricky fired, or how many are left in the mag, but there's at least 1 still unspent. I stand. Take 4 long steps along the bar.

"No, please, I'll do anything yo..."

BLAM! I buy Jamie a round.

5 short steps back—BLAM! I turn Tricky's head inside out.

There's a drift of snow on the marble counter. I resist the urge to shift into cocaine high gear, but I don't idle in pain either. Staggering to the *Magenta Room* I burst in, checking corners, but there's no 1 to shoot. By any standard the suite is palatial, it has its own lounge, dining area, and a hot tub balcony with a view across the river into East St. Louis—nice.

I take a moment to search the walk-in closet, finding it full of clothes and shoes and no monsters—unless you counted me—and a stack of freshly laundered Egyptian cotton bedsheets. In the bedroom, I throw the nickel .45 and the other Sig onto the silk bedspread, then return to the closet.

I selected an easy-fit tracksuit and sneakers and some fresh underwear, throw them next to the handgun, getting angry when the guns and clothes on top the silk bedspread spill onto the floor. Using my buckle knife, I nick every 4 inches or so along the hem of 1 cotton sheet and then tear strips to use for bandaging, carrying the makeshift dressings into the ensuite.

In the bathroom, a pink marble and gold taps affair, I gaze at the horror show that's my reflection in the full-length mirror. Behind the mirror is a cabinet, on a shelf are some Vicodin. I pop 2 and keep the bottle.

I don't wanna strip down, but I'm covered in death fluids, piss, and puke, and need to assess the GSW and my aching ribs. I dump the bandages on the washstand. Using the buckle knife, I cut away my shirt and peel the material carefully from the hole in my side—any foreign particles pushed into the wound are likely to suppurate, I need to clean it.

Even though it seems like forever, as time does when you're in the firing line, it can only have been 5 minutes tops since I got shot, but the blood has already started to ooze rather than flow, my body's natural coagulant trying to stem its loss. It hurts like a son of a bitch to lift my arm and look over my shoulder so I can assess the reflected damage of a surprisingly neat exit wound in the mirror—luckily, the bullet only hit soft tissue.

Blood leaks from the hole like discharge from a syphilitic cock, and about as pleasant to look at from my perspective. I pile my sodden clothes in the wash basket and pull out the cotton liner, thinking I'll dispose of the contaminated evidence later. I ain't a clothes horse, but I'm glad I didn't wear my Oxfords.

I'm pretty brutalized, but I got motion in the joints, nothing vital seems fucked up beyond repair, so long as I don't contract an infection, I think I oughta make it.

I set the dial to cold, even so, the shower burns hot on the open wounds afflicting my body. I shiver from pain and the chill. I'm tempted to lance the swelling 'round my left eye and drain the blood down the drain but think better of it. Instead, I push hard against my eye with the heel of my hand and flatten the bruise out a bit. I'll look for a pair of sunglasses in the walk-in before leaving.

Toweling down's a nightmare when you can't lift 1 arm above your head without suffering a bucketful of agony and a gush of fresh blood. I do my best to mummify the holes either side of my body with the bedsheet dressing—it won't pass inspection by matron, or anything, but the wrappings feel comfortingly tight. My abdominals and ribs look like tenderized veal, but nothing's broken. I touch my eye socket, there ain't any loose movement of bone, just a hard lump under the puffy bruising that feels like a bone-deep hematoma. I can wear that.

I dress, find some big-lens aviator shades, and head to the housekeeping utility closet off the main hallway. Parked just inside the door are 2 typical housekeeping trolleys for cleaning this level. On the shelf racking waits a year's supply of liquid bleach. I clear 1 trolley of brooms and mops and polish and load it with every bleach container I can find and a stack of towels. The executive floor's covered in my common DNA. 'Cause my leather gloves had been taken from me, my fingerprints are everywhere too—I intend to smudge or chemically contaminate as much of my presence as possible.

I snap on a pair of bright yellow rubber cleaning gloves and wheel the trolley along the main corridor to the secure anteroom. In the safe, I empty my grip of tools and wipe them over with towels and bleach, and anyplace I think I might have touched. I find my leather gloves inside the grip, I leave them in the bottom. My fake ID's in the corner with my baseball hat, I throw the ID in with the gloves and the hat in the wash basket liner with my bloodied clothes. All the tools are arranged in a heap on 1 metal shelf. My decision to take the cash to use as a bulletproof vest against any hitters who'd etch my name into a .22 bullet when the big boys discover I've taken out the top floor of their casino operation in more ways than decorative stands.

The space I make inside the grip I fill with about 10lbs in $100 bills, another 130lbs, give or take, I stuff into the trolley's laundry bin, and then haul the trolley back into the corridor. Then I haul the bodies littering the anteroom inside the safe using my functioning arm and a lot of expletives, muddying all that loose DNA into Frankenstein's monster of cross-contamination. The guns I collect in a mop bucket, wipe them and bleach them clean; no 1 will know who shot who or with what gun without a thorough ballistics reenactment. None of the guns are registered, at least not to me, and there ain't any prints on any of the weapons, and no CCTV of me rampaging through the penthouse, so I'm in the clear for multiple homicide—probably.

I can't open Rack's phone. Fingerprint and facial recognition—even the fingers on his severed hand—don't work and I don't got his password. Guys like us, we keep our secrets secret. Even with an IT digital crowbar, you can't get into my cell phones without some Einstein-level AI hacking device. I do, however, take my fucking wristwatch back. I gotta wipe off the blood on his muscle tee to see the dial, it's ticking time away reminding me to hurry the fuck up.

I throw the lopped-off body part in the safe with the rest of Rack. It's a shame I can't check the contact number given me by Duke against the call record and contacts saved on Rack's phone, but I only need 1 contact, 1 name I can negotiate a deal with to let me live without a permanent crick in the neck from looking over my shoulder—have you read Cormac McCarthy's *No Country for Old Men?* Great book, bad ending for 1 of the principal characters. I won't give away the plot, but I don't want none of that.

I bleach-bomb the safe interior until I'm giddy from the fumes, creating a forensic nightmare for any CSI mop squad. Satisfied I've done all I can, I lock the vault door and wipe all the surfaces free of prints.

In the corridor, I follow my blood trail with a bleach-soaked mop, wipe doorframes, then bleach down the ensuite bathroom, making sure I wipe the mop handle before leaving it in a running shower. Coming back through the *Magenta Room*

I'm tempted to just lie down on the bed and sleep, I'm so dog tired.

From the private lounge, mopped and sponged, I help myself to a bottle of Smart water and drink most of it in 1 go, my body dying to replace the fluids it's leaking. I stack 4 more bottles on top the trolley. After the adrenalin drains from my veins, everything becomes a Herculean effort. Every minor inconvenience inspires a raging tantrum that quickly fades into exhaustion. Doubts cloud my ability to think straight. I review my checklist for removing incriminating evidence and come up with a new list.

I do what I can, time slips away, I gotta get out.

Eventually, I get everything I'm taking with stacked next to the elevator and leave everything else to chance and the cleansing power of sodium hypochlorite.

Backtracking the route Rack always took to avoid camera surveillance, looking like a 90s mobster stereotype. I hide my exhausted limp with a pimp-roll in a borrowed tracksuit. Maybe the casino staff have seen plenty of these guys wandering 'round the back of house areas to turn a blind eye on 1 more bad motherfucker wearing sunglasses indoors and yellow rubber gloves, struggling to push a housekeeping trolley stacked with a leather grip full of money, a linin bag of soiled clothing, and the trolley trash bin and laundry bin bulging with a shit ton of used bills, because I bash through the corridors and elevator doors like I'm driving a bumper car at Six Flags and no 1 says a word.

I make it to my car. I gotta shift everything in the trunk about, get to the spare wheel and cut my personal cell phone out. Then I gotta reorganize the interior space, so the dirty laundered clean money and my dirty bloody laundry fits. I drop some bling from the C-Note haul in my pocket, wipe the trolley clean of prints, and park the thing in a bay next to the 1 I'm about to vacate.

Finally, I snap off my rubbers and fling them in the trunk. I almost wanna get caught by the time I pour myself into the driver's seat of my Kia, caught and treated for my injuries so I can close my non-fucked up eye and let medically approved opioids take me on a pain-free joyride. Almost, but not quite.

I sit for a minute and consider the least complicated exit strategy, requiring the least amount of energy. My mind's foggy, every alternative seems to require a fuck load of effort. I gotta go with what I got. Who knows, with a couple of hours rest, I'd maybe come up with a better alternative than the plan I'm currently working with. Given that my recent track record for good ideas is for shit, I doubt my ability to come up with anything better. With few options and fewer fluid ounces of blood than I'd arrived with, I do what I always do, duck and dive, bob and weave, slip and roll, and try not to get knocked on my ass.

The route I take to Erika's feels meanderingly indirect, but I get there. Park outside her building and using my personal cell phone get in touch with the only person alive in this city I hope might help me out here. On my burner, using the contact number I got from Duke, I make 1 more call and 1 final bet on the outcome of a desperate gamble.

"Mr. Black? This is Halo."

# 22.

3 days it takes me to move around without sucking pain through gritted teeth. During that time 8 men disappear without a trace and new management moves into St. Louis from Chicago. *The Furlough* casino is overseen, and refurbishment of the penthouse floor begins using discreet contractors to transform the distressed décor into something less jarring than the Pollock-esque splashes of red marbling, shattered glass floor mosaic and splintered woodwork, and the slaughterhouse mural plastering the walk-in safe and anteroom.

From a personalized medical kit, an essential emergency treatment paramedic bag I've added to over the years—for dealing with bumps and bruises from my fight days, and stab and bullet wounds for today—I treat myself with medical grade pain killers and antibiotics and authentic bandages in place of gritted teeth and bedsheets. I'd never been shot before, shot at, but never shot. I've seen plenty of GSWs; treated 1 or 2, lost 1 or 2 to infection or blood loss—that worried me. I ain't bleeding out; infection is the hidden killer. You can't beat bacteria in a fistfight, you gotta rely on meds and a drain. I got sufficient meds to see me through a week. I don't got a drain and wouldn't know how to attach 1 if I did.

At present, I'm surfing oxycodone, smearing Quick Clot, and swallowing Flucloxacillin. My right side is iodine yellow around the wound, my inside is whiskey golden around the pain. After cleansing the GSW site and checking for obvious foreign contaminates, my 'nurse' redresses the wound with hemostatic gauze bandaging.

Erika dry-heaves the 1st time she peels away the blood-soaked bed linin, sinks a gulp of whiskey from the neck of the bottle, and then 1st-aids an injury I oughta seek 2nd-aid treatment for if emergency room doctors ain't compelled to report walk-in gunshot casualties to the authorities. And no, I don't take a veterinarian hostage and force them to treat me like they do in the movies. And no, I don't got a shadowy international support network waiting in the wings to provide no-questions-asked assistance in return for a stack of gold coins. All I got to take care of my ills is a fighter's idea of anatomy, a fair grab-and-go EMT treatment kit, some past experience in bloody situations, and a very conflicted 1-night stand cum breakfast companion.

When Erika discovered me in semi-consciousness outside her apartment, I said, "Hey, I got shot, can you take me in and take care of me?"

And she said, "Sure, you don't need to ask, I'd do anything for you, Saint."

Did I and did she fuck say that. I lie my ass off until we're both in her apartment with the door's locked and my grip's sitting in the hall.

"I don't understand how you're so... well, fucked up, and your car doesn't have a scratch on it?" Erika states, wide-eyed and skeptical.

Hands on hips, under her leatherette jacket, she's wearing a lilac sleeveless jumpsuit with an elasticated drawstring pulling the material tight around her slim waist and wearing it well. If I hadn't lost a fair amount of blood, I'd have gotten a hard-on she looked so good. Her black heeled ankle boots make a Laural and Hardy sketch outta helping me up the stairs, now 1 boot's jinked 1 fiery hip into a disgruntled pose. I was in another fine mess, and I got some 'splaining to do.

"You look great," I flatter, the dark lenses of my ridiculous sunglasses giving Erika a Ray-Ban tan.

She brushes the complimentary distraction off, "You'd better tell me what the hell's going on, Saint?"

"You know what'll give that outfit an extra bit of sparkle?" I put my left hand in the left pocket of my horrible blue tracksuit jacket and pull out a very sparkly diamond earring and bracelet set; "Some ice."

She stands there, staring at the bribe, unimpressed.

"Have you just robbed a jewelry store or something?"

"Nooo, no, I don't boost stores or banks or anything like that," all the triple-stolen monies I got crammed into my grip and trunk don't count—not really.

She's having none of it, "Well...?"

"I recover certain items of worth and money owed to certain people that require a certain amount of discretion," I'm certain.

"Oh my God, you're a leg breaker for the mob."

"Nooo, no, not really. I'm a... a, kinda repo man."

"Bullshit, I should've known a guy like you wasn't in sales. I let you talk me out of my panties because I'm a dumb bitch when it comes to men. I can't do this, Saint... whatever this is?"

"Fair," I got it, I really did. Erika's a civilian, she don't belong in the world I operate in, why would someone I'd spent 1 night and shared 1 pancake breakfast with entangle their life in a car crash, metaphorical, they don't need to? "I'm sorry. It's just, I got no 1 else to turn to and I hoped... what did I hope? I hoped I could take advantage of your good nature for a few hours overnight... it's a selfish ask, I'll get outta your hair. I just need 1 favor?"

"What's that?"

"Can you carry my grip down to the car, I don't think I can make it without help."

Whether it's the orphan puppy tale, or my exhausted physical state, or my honesty, I don't know, but something mushes Erika's soft center.

"Are the police looking for you?"

"No, I'm cop free, I swear."

"OK, 1 night," she relents.

"For real?"

"Yeah, for real, you can stay 1 night... but I want you gone in the morning."

I ain't sure anyone's gonna be able to wake me in the morning, I'm so tired.

"Thanks, I appreciate it. Now that I'm staying, there is 1 more thing," I take the aviator's off and receive a shocked hand-to-mouth reaction at my facial contusion.

"I'll get an icepack for that."

"The eye can wait. What can't wait is, I need someone to change the dressing on my... wound..."

"What kinda wound?" she looks me up and down trying to guess from the hunched, limping, tracksuit-wearing physical wreck in front of her what the fuck needs urgent care.

"Kinda bullet wound."

Erika goes whiter than me, turns this information over in her mind for a beat, her eyebrows crease above her nose in stern thought, "Let me see those diamonds again."

## 23.

I sit in Erika's bathtub and bleed down the plughole while I'm bandaged with legit dressings, and then I sleep on a mattress cover made from garbage bags held in place by sticky tape. Every 4 hours for the 1st 24 hours, saturated dressings are changed for fresh wound cleanser dressings, checking for narcosis when the wound's exposed. I got a pack of sterile scalpels in the kit in case I gotta debride some dead flesh before it ruins the healthy tissue's healing process—easier said than done, I'm not sure Erika's up for that level of surgery. The skin 'round the entry and exit holes is angry, my right side swells into a violent purple bruise, but no thick, discolored, or oozing secretions leak from the hole like gangrene custard from a ring doughnut with a bullet hole center. For a day or so, I worry infection will get the better of me and I'll have to turn myself in or turn Erika's apartment into a morgue. Grateful for the advice given to me by my old mentor—*'Keep it clean and it won't go green'*—that potentially fatal bump in the road to recovery passes.

I gotta learn to wipe my ass with my left hand, and shaving's outta the question, so I grow a gruff jaw. Erika prepares all my meals and cuts them into bite-sized pieces. After the 1st night, when she threatens to barf at the sight of my innie-outie bullet hole, unexpectedly, she kinda enjoys her role as my private nurse, to the point she relents on her 1-night ultimatum and lets me bedrest for 3 nights. She also likes my budding beard, mostly because it hides 1/2 my face, she ribs. I'm too high on painkillers and booze to enjoy the personal attention of being bed-bathed, something my Johnson would usually respond to with full attention.

When the big fella halfheartedly starts to rise during 1 horizontal ablutions session, Erika, her new earrings glinting in the light, warns, in no uncertain terms, "None of that!".

Nursing me takes days off her actual job, lost earnings I'll reimburse with my weight from the penthouse safe money. Being pandered to is a novelty I could easily get used to, but I can't get used to getting shot. My brain agrees that it ain't keen on sharing my skull with a .22 slug, so the heavier cut of money I'll give up to Chicago. I could run, buy a new life, disappear somewhere hot, but all the money in the world can't buy peace of mind—paranoia, the fear that they're out to get you takes on another level when it ain't imagined.

On the night I'd killed and been half-killed at the casino, after I'd called Erika hoping some emotional blackmail would pressure her into subletting her place as an garbage bag ICU where I can rest up, I call the Chicago contact, the eponymous Mr. Black that Duke gave me, and pitch a deal that gives the lowdown on my 1-man murder spree, explaining as best I can the FUBAR situation and my intention to hand over the 3X stolen monies that was 1X stolen by Chicago and then by Tricky and C-Note, and then me. I coax a perception that I'm safeguarding the money in case the Feds show up and audit a vault full of unaccountable millions and dead bodies—nobody wants a RICO case on top of a multiple homicide investigation.

Of course, I tell a semi-lie. In part, I take the money to save it from possible governmental scrutiny, but mostly I'm holding onto a 130lbs bargaining chip to save me and Duke from physical rather than fiscal scrutiny—yeah, I ain't so mercenary that I'd leave my only real friend to drive around for the rest of his natural on false number plates while I keep shtum somewhere warm and secluded with a hot $6-million and change

Not that I can get through airport security with that much paper; I'd have to rent a private plane, and that would leave a trial. Not that I can fence that many $100 bills on the quiet, the word will go out that Chicago will pay high for information about its lost money. Probably cost me 1/2 the weight just to filter the cash into an escrow account. I could chance driving into Mexico and try to channel the cash there, but I don't hold a golden ticket punched by the cartels—so, I'd probably end up getting punched myself. The money's no good to me, I can't spend it 1 c-note at a time and walk around with $100 change in my pocket every time I wanna pack of cigarettes or gum. No, the best option, the healthiest all-round solution, is to take control before the only option is to hide.

A faceless voice on the end of the line listens silently: no threats, no raging, no recriminations, he just takes in what I say and responds with cold purpose.

"When do we get our money back?"

"I can't right now. Gimme a week to sort myself out."

"You got 3 days and then the deal's off and we'll collect what's owed in a less considerate way."

"Fair," I agree, I got no choice but to.

I ain't so naive to trust Chicago on the back of 1 phone call. If they find me during the 3 days I'm given, leniency will be dispensed with, and I'd be zip-tied to a chair… again. I got no doubt they'd be searching.

As soon as the call ends, I power down the burner in case the syndicate has someone on payroll who can triangulate my location from the cell towers its signal's pinging off.

I have time to replay in my head what's happened: the realization that Chicago used him, as well as used me, to cause friction between them and St. Louis and show their hand early in the game must've inspired Rack to weigh up his options, deciding to throw in with Tricky and throw me under the bus. The double-triple-crossing pygmy fucktard tipped Tricky off in Mutt and Yo-Yo's car when I followed him on the drive from his place to C-Note's, it's the only time I ain't with him after I save his life. I won't deny that I can be a nasty cunt when circumstances dictate, but I ain't a 2 or 3-faced son of a bitch or a snitch—that counts for something, right?

"You can't go out, you're still in pretty bad shape,"

Bad shape, I look like 100 miles of bad road in the bathroom mirror after I'd showered the side of my body with the usual amount of holes and dressed in my own clothes and Oxfords retrieved from the back of the Kia. A car I'd left parked in the street for 3 days and nights with 6-million skim and hustle money in the trunk.

Thankfully, Erika ain't the nosey type when I send her down to fetch the med kit and a change of clothing. As my old mentor once told me when I rock up in 1 to do a job with him: *'Tracksuits are for the track and time travelers from the 80s'*. Even though she's done me fair, I ain't the trusting kind. I watch from the apartment window as Erika shoves and wiggles her cute butt to move the linin bag of cash and lining bag of bloody clothes and humidor of cigars out the way of my 2nd grip. She must've realized what's stashed in the Kia's trunk, nothing else feels like the bulk of banded money in a loose bag, but she don't ask for details, the state of my appearance is enough of a visceral reality check that she don't wanna know what's-what any deeper than is necessary.

I'm developing quite a soft spot, on top of the hard-on I got for this woman. What was it she said about herself? *'It doesn't take much of a compliment for me to trust that someone's genuine.'* Well, I'm complimented by the few questions asked loyalty she's shown me.

The trouble with being a lone operator in all aspects of life is that you never really build strong bonds with other people, dependable bonds that don't break at the 1st inconvenience, let alone when you're up to your neck in complication. I got no solid friends in my life other than Duke and Bob, and Duke's in the wind until things calm down and I current relationship with Bob is through plexiglass. Who else would take a risk for me like Erika without demanding a big chunk of ill-gotten gains, no fucker else I know.

The effort just thinking about what I need to do is exhausting. There ain't nothing else for it, I gotta man up for a few more days. In a few more days I'd be fit enough to lay low in an outta the way motel on my own, but this ain't that day.

"I need to tie up a loose end and then I can get outta your hair," I explain to her, I'd been a burden to the max already.

She smiles like she means it, "I kinda like you in my hair."

I smile back, "If things go well, I can maybe stay a while longer, take you for a pancake breakfast?"

"I only eat pancakes after sex," 1 corner of her smile turns suggestive.

"Strawberry and banana, right?"

"You remember, I must have made an impression."

"All day, all night. I gotta get moving, see you later?"

"Be safe, OK?" her playful demeanor suddenly turns serious. And then she grabs me in a hug that don't squeeze hemoglobin jam outta the hole in my side, kissing me on the mouth until I almost change my mind about risking this meet; "For luck... I get the impression you need it today."

"As much as I can get."

I collect my keys and burner. My blackeye, having flattened out into a greeny-yellow discolored eyepatch, I cover beneath the aviator shades I'd indefinitely loaned from the casino's *Magenta Room*.

In the Kia, I drive a couple of blocks, find a dumpster, and dump the linin evidence bag full of evidence-soaked clothes. Then I park in a shopping lot a few blocks over, and move my personal shit onto the back seats, leaving the trunk full of millions of $s and an uninflated spare wheel with a flap cut into the underside of it.

Both my grips I'd left at Erika's, along with my real ID and personal cell phones. If I ain't around to buy her pancakes tomorrow for breakfast, she can have the 10lbs of cash I stowed in my leather grip, I wouldn't be needing it.

I choose a cigar and pocket C-Note's gold lighter. I got the Kimber 9 on the rider's seat next to me under a folded windbreaker I got out the trunk. The .45 Pitbull's stashed in the glovebox. If things go wild west, I want the shootout to go loud. The threat of an imminent 911 response to gunfire might be the only thing that saves my ass—but I doubt it. If I was a cat, I'd be down a couple of lives right about now, maybe on my last. I take a breath, power up the burner and Google map the city for neutral ground to schedule the meet. I laugh out loud when the search comes up with an ideal location.

"Halo?" the same no-nonsense voice who'd answered before picks up after the 3rd ring. He uses my AKA like a curse word.

I keep conversation short and to the point, "You want your money?"

"I'd appreciate it."

"Are you coming, or should I expect a friend of yours?"

"I'm in St. Louis taking care of the casino. I think you and me oughta meet."

"Alright, Mr. Black, Let's get this done."

"How d'you wanna do this?"

"Without complications."

## 24.

I pass through the Mackensie Road gate entrance and turn left at a base-mounted flagpole flying the stars and stripes behind the *Resurrection Cemetery's* granite name block. Cruise up to a small, blonde stone, red-roofed building with a cruciform pinnacle raised on its apex. There's parking behind. I pull in and take a tour of the building's exterior. It's locked. A plaque announces the building as the *St. Louis King of France Chapel.* I'm there, maybe 2 - 3 minutes, ample time to find a temporary nook to stash the ledgers I'd taken from C-Note's safe.

Jimmying myself between 2 privet bushes planted to screen a grey power box unit feeding electricity into the building, I find plenty of cover to hide the books and leave them hidden. I wriggle out and brush bushy dandruff from my clothes, taking a 360 to check if I'd be seen—it's clear.

I hop back into the Kia and turn right, leaving the chapel in my rearview mirror, meandering past decades-old gravestones to section 42, where a convenient stone bench is seated on the grass verge next to the paved roadway.

I park the Kia—again. Take my cigar and sit the bench looking out over a somber place of loss and remembrance. The meeting spot I choose is secluded enough to be private, yet open enough that I ain't the only living person around. It's a nominal precaution that may or may not give a cagey man pause to commit terminal violence, and

I get the impression that Mr. Black is a very guarded gangster who positions himself at a distance by 3 - 4 removes from the ruthless activities that fund his lifestyle. But, for all his cautious insolation, he is an ambitious gangster who rose up through the ranks of an uncompromising criminal organization and was made a boss, so maybe in the next hour his crew will bury me in 1 of the cemetery's open plots for taking liberties with the money and the casino and the St. Louis crew?

Using my buckle knife, I cut a notch in its cap, lighting the cigar foot with an even burn from my new gold lighter. It's fair weather, too warm for a windbreaker, but I wear it to cover the bulge of the Kimber tucked in my waistband. Mr. Black's sure to come heavy and in numbers. 1 kiss for luck ain't gonna keep me from being ventilated—again. I'm an existing inconvenience, I'll have to convince the Chicago boss that making a deal is a smarter play than erasing my existence all together.

I carry the gun like a comfort blanket, and maybe to prove that I ain't gonna cause no more grief when I give it up. The element of surprise is gone, the guys Black will bring will be seasoned hitters, their hands will be on their weapon of choice, and they won't be shoveling snow up their noses. I'm a warmonger waving a flag of truce—if peace ain't granted, then the shortest war in history will be declared and fought and ended before I mobilize resistance.

Halfway through the cigar, I hear the low growl of 2 black Town Cars approaching from the north. My heart delivers an adrenalin bump. I ditch the stogie and suck in a few breaths to calm myself, it feels like the buildup to a no-holds-barred bareknuckle fight.

On the phone, I told Black to look out for a blue Kia Soul. He snorted at that, his kind of G is unapologetically judgmental over the car you drive, the guns you carry, the clothes you wear, the race you're born into, and the places, other than your traditional mob wife or side-chick, you stick your prick.

2 black sedans pull in next to my Soul and the doors of the lead car wing, spreading 4 serious-looking men onto the grass verge and roadside. They scan about, checking this ain't a setup of some kind, and then 1 of them, a big guy with an unfriendly bulge in his pants, probably a .45 revolver, steps up to where I'm waiting—non-threateningly.

"Stand," he orders, the others got his back, hands near where their heaters rest coldly against their hips.

I do as I'm told, raising my arms in anticipation of a pat down. The Kimber's found and taken, my lighter and car keys are left in my pockets. My burner cell's confiscated, and covert listening devices hunted for—our private talk is gonna remain private if Mr. Black has anything to do with it.

The goon don't find my belt knife, securely clipped behind the buckle, it's some consolation to personal protection, but not much. Lastly, he asks for my sunglasses, grinning appreciatively at the bruising they hide when I hand them over—I guess Black wants to look me in the black eye to better assess the substance of my words.

I'm ushered over to the 2nd car. The goon opens the door and holds it, the driver exits.

"Back seat," it ain't an invitation.

The dice are thrown. I got no more chips in the game. It's a breakeven or lose everything type bet—the kinda risk only a degenerate gambler would chance. The kinda loose play that got me on Casey's back and subsequently got his toes turned into bloody flippers a week ago in Vagas—fuck, only a week.

The leather squeals when I sit into the Lincoln's seat cushion to the left of a balding, black-rinsed, blue-eyed, vain, spaghetti-twister, in a dark-grey suit tailored to flatter the paunch he's trying to hide, and blue-silk tie dignifying his position as a boss. And then the big guy closes the door on the world, insulating our interaction mano a mano.

Straight off, I know who I'm sitting next to. His face has been linked to organized crime, hitting the headlines whenever an indictment slides his way before he and his attorneys slip outta any conviction. Black's an alias, an AKA for the purpose of our relationship, an AKA he continues with, and I keep to.

The new casino manager barely looks my way, as if I'm a bug on the windshield rather than a thug in the car, "I'm a man who's witnessed violence. Been on 1 end or the other from time to time, but what you left behind 3 days ago was a fucking bloodbath," he accuses, not wrongly.

"Yeah, I kinda got overcommitted."

"Overcommitted? My men had to dig more fucking graves in the Daniel Boons than there are in this fucking cemetery," this time he exaggerates, but his embellishment's fair, considering.

"I got cornered. I should've walked the moment the job was offered, but I got bills to pay."

He nods at that truth, a man with responsibilities to collect and distribute ill-gotten gains, "How much d'you know about the contract to look into Tricky and C-Note?" he don't fucking swear this time, this time he's gauging how much of a problem I might be.

"Just that: take a look at the casino, see if I can find the leak, report back. The job was setup through 3rd parties."

"Leak… it was a fucking flood, and now it's costing a lot more. I've got my own 3rd parties fitting new carpets throughout the penthouse and C-Note's home office. His wife had to be persuaded to keep quiet, it seems all her jewelry has fucking disappeared. I think she's more pissed at that than you staining the rug with her husband's shit for brains."

"The jewelry's gone: exchanged for medical." I kinda half-truth, Erika's my medical care, and she's wearing the exchange in her earlobes and on her wrist.

"Didn't go all your own way, then?"

"Not so much. I don't know if what happened sorted out a bad situation you guys had with Tricky and C-Note or if I made things worse, you're the best judge of that. But I'm here to cut a simple deal that don't make any more complications for you."

"How much of a deal," Black looks at me then, looks me dead in the eye.

Through the windows into his soul, deep into the dark recesses of his Machiavellian consciousness, I see a glint of avarice—the golden idol of all crime bosses.

Then I know without speculation, that this motherfucking schemer's the origin of all my pains. Without doubt, it was Mr. Fucking Black who started the engine and let the juggernaut go; more than willing to let a subcontractor—me—get crushed in the wreckage if his plan hit a sinkhole in the road, and more than happy to steal the glory, and the lion's share of the recovered skim, if the juggernaut smoothed the road ahead for his takeover. A hostile takeover where I'm the hostile and he and his crew ain't taken so much as a scratch from the opposition or any negative press from his own organization.

C-Note was written into the syndicate's books, a legit under-boss, maybe not as high status as Black, but someone who had connections—he'd have to get caught transacting some seriously disloyal business or get fingered as a rat before an OK to remove him from the picture would be given. Tricky was different, he'd be considered a pervert-homo by most of the syndicate's alpha Gs. It wouldn't take much for them to cancel a bugger like Tricky if his tenure as their moneymaker at the casino failed to cash out ahead.

I guessed C-Note had Tricky in his pocket and was protecting him from the phobics in his organization. More than likely, he vouched Tricky into the manager's position so he could take advantage of the setup. That was a problem. Someone was sus about what was going on, and that someone was Mr. Black.

If the man I'm sitting next to burned the St. Louis operation and its operators, then he, and he alone, would be liable for the loss in income to the whole organization. But if word spread that Tricky and C-Note and some local Gs got into a dubious unsanctioned enterprise that ended in 'chaos', then tying off the hemorrhaging money vein, and stabilizing the disruption to business that a multiple homicide investigation would bring, would be considered a problem that Black had solved.

After my call informed him that St. Louis' top tier had been dropped, he swept in as damage control and cleaned house—literally—hid the bodies, covered up my, his, Rack's, involvement, so he can line his own pockets while reporting to Chicago that their laundering service is back in the black and their casino is once more pumping out green.

"Around 6-mil," I estimate.

A twitch of a smile, and then it's gone, "You didn't count it?"

"With only 1 good arm? The weight feels about right."

As a man who'd lumped bags of cash around, he nods understanding, "You lose any weight from the casino to here?"

"Just the jewelry and some gas money," I'm letting him know that I ain't a devotee of avarice like him, just a bow-the-head believer in the criminal faith.

"My cleaners tell me you did a good job with the bleach, but you would've missed something incriminating with that much carnage. Don't worry, there won't be anything substantiating that'll tie you to what happened after we finish refurbishing the top floor. Any residual fingerprints'll be under a fresh coat of paint by now?"

"Gonna take a few tubs of Polyfilla to patch up all the holes."

"Not before my decorator digs out the brass and lead for scrap value."

"Yeah, I hear there's good money in scrap."

"There's money in all types of dirty work if you can stand the grime. I can use someone off the books who don't mind getting their hands dirty from time to time, if you're interested."

"You've already made use of me."

He hmphs a dry laugh, "You only work through a go-between?"

I nod.

"I can give your guy a taste to keep the relationship alive?"

Alive? He's fishing, there's subtext in the offer, bait I ain't taking.

"I'm taking a trip south of the border," I lie, I'm heading west, about 8700 miles west; "I don't think I'll be back this way any time soon."

"So, we won't be seeing each other again?"

"Never."

"Never say never, Halo."

"I got nothing keeping me in Illinois and plenty of reasons to keep me away."

"Couple of thousand reasons, I oughta think?"

I ain't owning that, but Black knows himself and by association knows the type of man sitting next to him—we hustle.

"I don't wanna hear about you working for anyone else in my organization."

"You won't."

There's an old saying: *'Keep your friends close and your enemies closer'* – my motto is – *'Keep your friends at arm's length and your enemies as far away as possible'.*

"Where's the weight now?"

"Trunk of the Kia," I dangle the key.

"You brought with?"

"Yeah, as a gesture."

"And the ledgers?" he's speculating that the ledgers I found at C-Note's are full of markers and payments and contacts that will weigh as much again and keep the interest rolling in.

"Insurance. I'll give you a location where they're at when I'm on the road. I'll make the call, then my cell's wiped along with the sim card and call records. It'll be as if I was never here."

Black's mulling the pros and cons. He and his crew have just drained a 'bloodbath' on the Mississippi. Is it worth digging another unmarked grave to make me give up the ledgers when I'm offering them freely—with a little distance between to ensure pleasantries continue.

"You mentioned a name: a payoff at the Building Division's Examiner's Office keeping the problem land reports buried."

It's my turn to mull over the pros and cons of whether I oughta hold 1 last bargaining chip back, "Gary Dursley," I spill.

Mr. Black nods. He buzzes the window down, takes the car key from my hand, and gives it to frisker, "Take the cash from the Smurf-mobile's trunk and leave the key in the ignition, Mr. Halo's taking a road trip south of the border."

His goon does as he's instructed, leaving the items he'd taken from me on the rider's seat.

We don't shake hands. The money's incentivizing, but the payoff name and the ledgers, assuming they could break C-Note's scrambled code—I couldn't—sweeten the deal. Mr. Black would be too busy counting his winnings and consolidating C-Note's budding criminal empire to give me a 2nd thought in the foreseeable. But I ain't complacent about my side of the deal, paranoia has put a bullet in the back of someone's skull more times than a breakfast pancake has strawberries.

Anyway, I'm alive. I got enough gas money to get me far away from Illinois, and enough spending money to enjoy the sights and sounds of Thailand without roughing it like a gap year student on a rice and noodles budget. I won't be sending any postcards, so good luck finding my tanned ass.

# 25.

28 hours on an airplane via Chicago O'Hare International and Hamad International is quicker than swimming to Phuket Island, but it seems just as slow, no matter how many inflight movies you watch, when you're desperate to feel warm sand between your toes and gentle surf up your calves. A conveyor belt of Old Fashions sedates me into a light buzz, and a pulp fiction crime thriller distracts my attention for a couple of 100 pages. By the time we're descending, I'm ready to jump from the plane if someone offers me a parachute landing.

In part, my impatience stems from a lack of opportunity to vent my frustrations, my temper, and my testosterone over the past 2 weeks while I healed—not the phycological healing process beta bleaters whine on about, but real fucking physical booboos that remind you that you ain't immortal.

Sex helped. But it ain't brutal enough to pour all my pent-up energy into—sometimes you need a night of cruel fucking to calm the raging storm. Even though my injuries won't permit top-level bed jujitsu, I can wrestle some interesting moves on the mattress. The plug scar in my side gives me a stab of pain whenever I do a pushup, and I'd lost enough mobility on my right side that I can't stretch the hang of a pullup yet, and the bastard thing itches all the time, but I'm getting stronger day by day.

By the time I'm long-distance reclining in an airplane seat, I've recovered enough from my hurts that I crave the endorphin release of some serious regular training. The last time I sparred or lifted or blasted cardio was before the Vegas job. Although physically demanding, the stand-up fight I'd gotten into at *The Furlough* don't count as feel-good exercise. 15 years hitting the weights, hitting the pads, hitting sparring partners has ingrained my mind, body, and spirit with addictive needs. I'm an adrenalin junkie, a risk-taker, a thrill-seeker, a physical motherfucker cooped up in an aluminum tube with wings.

My accommodation and travel arrangements—Qatar Airways flight from St. Louis Lambert International Airport arriving at Phuket International Airport, Terminal 2, Phuket Island, Thailand—is organized with 2 days research and 1 day of booking, but I had to stop limping and bleeding and swelling before I can walk through airport security without drawing attention to myself, so I keep my head down and hang out for 3 weeks in St. Louis, growing fat on pancakes and meds and whiskey, and converting a weighty bag of $ clippings into digital green.

I email Duke through our emergency contact, let him know that he can drive his beloved car with its own plates again. We get new burners and make a call. My middleman's full of questions I ain't answering, and I don't tell him the amount of my compensation or what I plan to do with it, but I do gotta ask him for a trusted guy who'll flip cash into a numbered account.

"Yeah, I know a guy who can do that," he confirms.

"A guy, not a name?"

"He's the one sets up our escrows; been solid up to now."

"OK, give his details."

We shoot the shit for a few, he asks when I'll be available for some yard work, I tell him I'm taking a sabbatical.

"But you're good, through?" he worries, after I tell him about my new hole.

"Yeah, I'm good on 1 side and getting there on the other."

"Be good, Halo."

"Keep your dukes up, Duke."

We hang up.

A smudge of concealer, applied by Erika, hides my facial bruises from notice when I go out and about to set things in motion and to meet Duke's escrow Guy. The bruises fade in a week, my face just looks more tired on 1 side than the other.

Luckily, I don't need any dental work, so when I smile at the airport check-in staff, I don't look like a crystal meth hillbilly chewing a baccy wad. All I want now, is to settle into the villa I've long-term rented, explore the beach and bars where I've chosen to stay, sip a few cocktails, and then find a Thai boxing gym to start a fitness regimen that ain't interrupted by travel, or work, or avoiding the cops, or dodging hitmen.

From the *Suntimes* villa company's online options menu, I shell out additional money from 1 of my new online accounts for a food and amenities welcome pack to be arranged in the villa when I arrive. On top of that, I engage cleaning and laundry services for the duration of the stay—yeah, I'm gonna live it up on the lowdown. Once I get my local bearings, I'll rent a car, so I'll be self-reliant. Once I get used to Thai traffic, I'll explore farther afield. For today, though, I'll get around by cab, tuk-tuk, and bus.

Disembarkation is smooth. Breezing through baggage collection and security (what there is of it) like a regular person with regular travel documents and IDs—which is a novelty considering I've been wearing Halo for so many years that it takes me by surprise every time someone calls me by my given. Wheeling a baggage trolley loaded with 1 luggage grip, 1 well-kept leather grip, 2 brand new suitcases, and a manbag strapped across 1 shoulder, kinda reminds me of wheeling the housekeeping trolley through the casino, although, on this occasion, I'm fit to vacation rather than fit to drop as I swagger through customs—nothing to declare.

I set my Tag Heur to local time. In my manbag is a wedge of 15,000 Thai Baht, that's around $430, so I ain't loaded down with cash. I use some of the monies I gave myself as a commission for getting shot and shooting dead 3, suffocating 2, hacking and hammering another 3, and pistol-whipping 1 woman, for runaround gas, and nearly a month of pancake breakfasts, the rest of the weight I get laundered into an escrow that I'll drip-feed over time into the numbered accounts I already got setup.

Although bundled in inconvenient $10,000 straps of a 100 $100 bills, having been washed through the gaming floor, the casino cash is already clean and nonsequential, so I only needed to pay 4 points on 11lbs AKA 500 liters AKA 500Gs AKA 1/2 a mil, to the guy who transferred it from a weight of 75% cotton and 25% linen 'paper' into numbered accounts of digital weightlessness, which leaves a sum total of $480,000, plus my $150,000 savings, to live like a boss for a few years.

The villa I choose is a 2-bed with a pool near Rawai beach on the south-eastern side of Phuket Island for $2,200 a month—that's around 250 thou a decade, with 380l all told for gas. As I plan to live more than another 10 years, and plan to have fun while I'm doing it, I'll have to boost my retirement fund if I want other people to wash my underwear and clean up my mess and maintain my pool. I ain't settled permanent, I'll probably move around, explore other places and lifestyles. For now, though, forget about it.

From scrolling the internet and reading a bunch of travel reviews, Rawai fits the bill for the right now and foreseeable. Off-the-beaten-track, with training centers devoted to Muay Thai at all levels, from absolute kick to the head beginners to kick the head world champions. The heat, humidity, and Thai massages oughta help loads with my flexibility rehab. There's abundant social life to cater for dining out, drinking out, and laying out on golden sands. 1 reviewer I read wrote that their visit to Rawai Beach was a *'Transformative experience'*—sold.

Into the balmy heat of the airport pick-up and drop-off zone, I hail a yellow minivan with large passenger windows along the side panels for tourists to take in the view. The driver assures me he knows the route to Rawai and where Sai Yaan Road villas are. We barter a price for the trip—45 minutes of twisting roads and beautiful scenery—settling on 1,340 Thai Baht ($30) from airport to front door.

After 30 minutes we're cruising along a golden stretch of sand with palm trees and blue surf that makes what will become my local beach appear like a Photoshopped Garden of Eden. I cut a wedge in the head of a cigar with my buckle knife, reclaimed from luggage on arrival, and take a deep inhalation along a tightly rolled cylinder of Cuban leaf. I'll light up using my reclaimed gold lighter when we arrive at our destination.

On the journey over, I call the villa agent on 1 of my 3 cell phones—he introduces himself as Pakorn. An affable middle-aged Thai man meets the minivan as it pulls up to my new home from home, he's small in stature but impeccably presented in a *Suntimes* logoed white shirt and green shorts.

I slide from the seat into balmy sunshine and stick a C-Note cigar in my mouth, I'm gonna enjoy the fuck outta this moment—my dream has become reality, and all it took was partnering the Grim Reaper on a soul harvest and almost joining the crop we reaped.

"Mr. Greaves, welcome, welcome," the *Suntimes* agent greets, raising his hands palms together to his face and bowing.

"Hi, Pakorn, looks amazing," I praise around the unlit cigar, lifting my hand to emphasize the front of a pristine white villa with a paved path cutting across a neat little garden leading to the front door—my front door.

"Beautiful, just like the online pictures," agrees my housemate.

Giving another deep bow, "Thank you. And this is Mrs. Greaves?" the agent enquires of the very attractive short-haired brunet holding hands at my side.

I take the waiting cigar from my lips and smile, "My nurse, Erika."

END

$10,000
$10,000
MP 10033014 P
K2
100
MP 10033014 P
100
100

Printed in Great Britain
by Amazon

36703347R00124